D1042158

THE
LOVE PROOF

THE
LOVE PROOF

— A Novel —

MADELEINE HENRY

ATRIA BOOKS

NEW YORK   LONDON   TORONTO   SYDNEY   NEW DELHI

ATRIA
BOOKS

An Imprint of Simon & Schuster, Inc.
1230 Avenue of the Americas
New York, NY 10020

First Atria Books hardcover edition February 2021

ATRIA BOOKS and colophon are trademarks of Simon & Schuster, Inc.

For information about special discounts for bulk purchases, please contact
Simon & Schuster Special Sales at 1-866-506-1949 or
business@simonandschuster.com.

The Simon & Schuster Speakers Bureau can bring authors to your live event. For
more information or to book an event, contact the Simon & Schuster Speakers
Bureau at 1-866-248-3049 or visit our website at www.simonspeakers.com.

Interior design by Jill Putorti

Manufactured in the United States of America

1 3 5 7 9 10 8 6 4 2

Library of Congress Cataloging-in-Publication Data

Names: Henry, Madeleine, author.
Title: The love proof / Madeleine Henry.
Description: First Atria Books hardcover edition. | New York : Atria, 2021.
Identifiers: LCCN 2020020280 (print) | LCCN 2020020281 (ebook) |
ISBN 9781982142964 (hardcover) | ISBN 9781982142988 (ebook)
Subjects: GSAFD: Love stories. | Science fiction.
Classification: LCC PS3608.E5736 L69 2021 (print) | LCC PS3608.E5736
(ebook) | DDC 813/.6—dc23
LC record available at https://lccn.loc.gov/2020020280
LC ebook record available at https://lccn.loc.gov/2020020281

ISBN 978-1-9821-4296-4
ISBN 978-1-9821-4298-8 (ebook)

for Dave,
my love beyond time
and space

"When connections are real, they simply never die. They can be buried, or ignored or walked away from, but never broken. If you deeply resonated with another person or place, the connection remains despite any distance, time, situation, lack of presence, or circumstance . . . Real connections live on forever."

—Victoria Erickson, author of
Edge of Wonder and *Rhythms and Roads*

PART ONE

CHAPTER 1

Before they met, Jake Kristopher was sitting in the third row of Woolsey Hall, Yale's biggest auditorium, glancing up at the balcony behind him. Woolsey was packed with teens dressed up for freshman assembly, on the energetic brink of their first college semester. Sophie Jones was craning forward over the balcony rail when Jake caught a glimpse of her and went still. She had golden hair and wore a white dress with a bumblebee woven on one shoulder. As people around her chatted, she sat alone. She looked younger than everyone else. The longer he stared, the more his feeling swelled that he'd seen her before—no, more than that. Known her.

Sophie found his gaze in the crowd. His black eyebrows were knit together, dark as ocean depths. Her stomach fluttered as if he were a tide pulling her under with him. The jock next to him suddenly turned around and blocked her view with the width of his shoulders. Sophie leaned back, dropped her hand to her gut, and wondered why she'd felt such a charge.

*　　*　　*

"Is it Soph*ie* or Soph*ia*?" Professor Ali Kotak asked, slanting toward Professor Peter Malchik. They sat an inch apart at the Yale Physics Department meeting. Her name, of course, was Sophie Jones—"The Next Einstein," according to the *New York Times*'s profile. In that piece, the three most decorated mathematicians in the world had predicted *she* would be the one to answer humanity's legendary questions about space and time within the decade—the most profound, undefeated ones about *what reality is*, with transformative implications for mankind.

"Sophie," Peter whispered casually.

His Yale-blue bow tie stood out in the room of wrinkled button-downs and rayon polos. Peter was an angular man with prominent knuckles, elbow joints, and kneecaps. He exhibited perfect posture in the drowsy meeting, where everyone faced the chair, a hefty Russian astrophysicist named Pavel Kapitsa, speaking at the head of the table. Meanwhile, Peter tapped his blue pen on the notebook open in front of him, flecking blue confetti, and thinking eagerly, tensely, about how close he was to meeting her after waiting so long.

". . . She elected to study time," Pavel droned, his voice deep. " 'How can we see time?' "—Pavel bent his fingers into crisp air quotes—"is her stated research question. Peter will be her advisor, but she'll run into everyone here at one point or another, and she may approach any of you." Pavel gave Peter an expectant look, his stare soft under snowy eyebrows.

"Now?" Peter asked.

Pavel nodded and motioned for him to stand. Peter rose as tall as he could at five foot seven. His thin cheeks stretched as he forced a smile, though he didn't care much for the men and women around him. Most people irked him. He thought Sophie would be an exception. Ever since she'd committed to Yale last winter, she'd become a visual earworm. Sometimes it was her face that came to him: unusually blonde hair in sinusoidal waves down to her waist, her expression cool, contemplative. Peter had a habit of thinking in shapes, which improved his natural memory tenfold. Sometimes he saw her as an apeirogon, a polygon with infinite sides. On the black stage of his mind, she appeared as a bright, magnificently intricate disco ball, with dazzling complexity and limitless potential.

Last year, Sophie had aced the International Mathematical Olympiad—the top math tournament for high schoolers—for the fourth time in a row. The IMO had drawn the most gifted students to compete annually since the 1950s. No one else had earned a perfect score four times. Only one other had aced it three times. Sophie's world record had ignited a global news cycle featuring her as a prodigy: front-page newspaper articles, including the *Times*'s "The Next Einstein," and TV interviews, including four minutes on *Good Morning America*. Peter had a fan's grasp of her already. From clips, he knew her voice was childlike. Her manner was vulnerable, sweet. Every answer she gave was gentle and . . . feminine. A girl. There weren't many at her level of scientific thought, and no one else so young.

She was so docile, so *un*-intense, that her success seemed to be through no will of her own and instead supernatural. She often tilted her head to the side, seemingly absorbed in something else entirely, as if she straddled reality and a dream. Her long hair added to the mystical quality.

"Hello," Peter said. "Pavel's asked me to speak about how I'll be working with Sophie. She's been enrolled in a new course, an advanced tutorial, where we'll be working one-on-one. The plan is to meet once a week for two hours. In between, I'll assign ten problems, all on time theory. We'll discuss her solutions together. As Pavel said, she wants to answer the question, 'How can we see time?' "

Everyone saw the evidence that time was passing—clocks ticked, seasons changed—but Sophie wanted to see time itself. In her college essay describing what she would study at Yale, she'd asked: "*What* exactly is passing, and *where* is it? How can we see time?" She cited Albert Einstein. In 1905, Einstein had introduced the concept of special relativity, the breakthrough understanding that the three dimensions of space were fused with time in a seamless, four-dimensional fabric. So, as Sophie wrote in her essay, "If space and time are fused in a continuum, why can we see space but not time?" Matter is observable to the naked eye and reduces to atoms. Light, too, is visible—from red all the way to violet—and reduces to photons. "Why not time?" The question lay in Peter's area of expertise. He'd been studying time for the past decade at Yale while teaching the school's only class on the subject. In the process, he'd become the world's most published expert on time theory. He'd opined most extensively on the possibility of traveling back in time. He'd argued in major journals that it was possible to do so through a wormhole, a theoretical tunnel connecting different regions of space-time.

"What's so special about her?" Peter's son Benji had asked at dinner last night.

Peter prodded his fusilli.

"You like video games, right?" he asked.

His wife, Maggie, glared at him across the table.

"Yeah," Benji said.

"Okay, imagine the most difficult, the most awesome game you know," Peter said. "Imagine the highest level in that game, the one you've never been able to pass. Now, imagine you meet someone who's a better player than you. She can pull off moves you can only dream of—triple-axel over enormous mushrooms—"

"Whoa," Benji said.

"But she's never played this game before," Peter went on. "She's asked you to coach her just a little bit. And the more you learn about her, the more excited you get because you know, really know, that with your help, she'll not only pass the highest level you've ever seen, she will win the game."

Back in the meeting, Pavel motioned for him to sit.

"Thank you, Peter," he said. "When's your first session?"

"Today."

*　　*　　*

Jake ran into the lecture hall and scanned for a seat. Hundreds of open laptops dared class to start. Their cursors pulsed like pinned clock hands. Conversations—lively, still buzzing with icebreaker questions—dwindled into attentive silence. Jake lifted the collar of his black tee away from his chest and fanned himself with it. He was squinting at the professor below when he spotted a familiar head in front. On instinct, he strode toward her, passing ponytails like pendulums.

"Excuse me," Jake apologized as he cut across the front row. In the center, Sophie was leaning forward and resting her pen on her bottom lip. Her tight red tee clung to her chest. Her jean shorts were patterned with bright sequined shapes—purple star, green moon, butterfly with two antennae—and fringed at the hem. The outfit seemed oddly young, as if it were meant for someone half her age. When she glanced up at the shuffling noises, Jake waved. His gut feeling about her was stronger now. He had the sense they'd shared something important. He couldn't remember what, but it had made them similar, as if they'd both been wounded by the same thing. They had been fragile together. They had survived something.

He sat next to her and smiled kindly.

Wait, Sophie thought. *How do we . . . ?*

PowerPoint slides changed. Sophie faced forward but peeked sideways as he opened his laptop. The man's muscles were etched like ones in an anatomy textbook: from the deltoid capping his shoulder, to the paired biceps and triceps, to the smaller brachioradialis and flexor carpi on his forearm, and then countless blue veins. Sophie had never seen a harder body. She liked the way it looked alive. His black tee waved at the neckline, suggesting years of being yanked off overhead, big thumbs stretching the stitches.

Oh. Sophie raised a blonde eyebrow so faint it was nearly invisible. *From assembly?* That didn't feel like the full answer. His smile had shown more recognition than that. He had looked happy to see her. She kept peeking at him. He didn't take many notes. When he did type something, it was a quick clack just a few words long. Still, she could tell he was listening, deeply rooted in this moment. He seemed more grounded than other students scribing every word, as if he had a keen sense for what was important.

This Introduction to Psychology lecture had packed the house. The professor asked a series of questions describing the course. Topics included the brain, dreams, love—"What makes someone attractive? What makes two people fall in love?"—sex and morality, each detailed in a preview. Jake didn't believe the professor had answers to any of these fundamental questions of existence—who did?—but he stayed for the girl beside him. When the professor finished, thin applause broke out in pockets. Jake, hands on his keyboard, waited as she slipped her notebook into her backpack stuffed with hardcovers.

Sophie had her first meeting with Professor Malchik that afternoon. He'd sent their syllabus that morning, so Sophie knew that today, they would discuss the origin of time. Most physicists agree that space and time were created in the big bang almost fourteen billion years ago. For the first 10^{-43} seconds of history, the universe fit into a space smaller than a proton. All four fundamental forces—gravity, weak interaction, strong interaction, and electromagnetism—were unified in conditions so strange and incomprehensible that no one has yet described them with any physical laws. At 10^{-43} seconds, gravity split from the other three forces, and the universe as we know it began to take shape.

As Sophie zipped her backpack shut, she was half thinking about the start of everything and half hoping she and this man would leave at the same time.

She slung her arms through the straps.

"Hey," Jake said.

He towered over her at six foot four. Sophie smiled for a moment shorter than 10^{-43} seconds before they moved in step with the crowd.

"I'm sorry, how do we . . . ?" she asked.

Her question lingered as he opened the door for them. It destabilized his comfort with her. Why *did* he feel like they'd shared a history? On the sidewalk, they stopped and took each other in. Jake's gaze dropped to the inch of skin between her shirt and shorts. Her short nails were painted white. The bracelets up her arms—unsculpted, soft—were beaded with different phases of the moon, with a sunlike orb in the middle. A starfish glinted in the V-dip of her silver necklace chain. Her face was so bare, Jake saw something Aphroditic in her, as if she'd emerged from something as natural as sea-foam. Sophie took in Jake's dark hair, tan, and brown eyes. He had a big nose. His lean cheeks pointed to a sharp, clean chin. Up close, she saw something undeniably sober, thoughtful about him. It was in his posture—straight back, low shoulders, balanced—this sense of purpose.

Sun warmed their skin as they stood. Particles of light bounced between them. Some of these specks had just come from the sun, through ninety-three million miles of the galaxy in eight minutes; past stars, planets, and through gas, dust, and empty black soundlessness before touching them. Jake and Sophie stood three steps apart, their bodies connected by light.

"You were at the assembly. I'm Jake."

"Sophie."

To her own surprise, she extended her hand. Sophie didn't usually feel this comfortable with strangers. The past few days, swarms of unfamiliar people at every turn had inhibited her even more than usual. But here she was. He asked where she was headed. She glanced at her watch: 2:15 p.m. She had to meet Professor Malchik at three.

"Dining hall?" she suggested.

He nodded.

As they walked, they learned that they hadn't, in fact, met before assembly and started from zero with their questions. Jake was from New York City, Sophie from Westchester. They were both only children—Sophie brightened when she heard that.

At the moment of Sophie's double take, one-half mile away, Peter sat in his office reviewing his notes. Her syllabus was on his round table. Peter had dug outside the scope of time theory to build his lesson plan, including ideas from astrophysics, biology, chemistry, and psychology to create a spectacularly cross-discipline, one-of-a-kind course. He'd also read about who Sophie might be and how she might learn. How should he coach a prodigy? What were her particular needs? Weaknesses? Peter had read about gifted children in journals, newspapers, and magazines, expensing every new subscription to the Physics Department.

By now, he thought he had a sense for Sophie, without ever having met her. About half of Americans were lonely. Among overachievers, as he learned, that percentage was higher. The statistics had made instant sense to him. Oddly, learning about widespread loneliness had made him feel momentarily less alone. Several studies reported that roughly 55 percent of American adults said they felt like no one knew them well. They lived alone, had major interests they didn't share, or worked all day in solitary professions. Whole parts of their lives were invisible. About 50 percent of adults said their "relationships weren't meaningful," and their ties to others were "superficial." Against that bleak landscape, eighteen-to-twenty-one-year-olds who identified as overachievers had the fewest social connections. Half of straight-A students in college went at least one day a week without having a conversation.

People like Sophie weren't used to intimacy. He wondered if she even realized how lonely she was, given that she knew nothing else. Starting today, she'd be with him for hours every week, receiving his full attention. He glanced at his wall clock—

2:30 p.m.—while inside Silliman dining hall, Jake and Sophie claimed seats across from each other at a long table. Arched windows taller than Jake lined the walls. Chandeliers that invited comparisons to Hogwarts lit the high ceiling. Sophie studied Jake's heaping bowl of Cheerios.

"Great minds . . ." He pointed to the waffle on her plate.

"You hate lunch or love breakfast?"

"I feel like I just woke up."

He clearly meant it in the most energetic sense of the phrase. He unclenched both fists like eyes opening to a new day. On the bottom row of his smile, Sophie noticed his teeth overlapped. His top two teeth slanted toward each other, too. She liked that he had a physical flaw. Her heart moved. Jake held up two large fingers and waved them.

"Hm?" Sophie asked.

He lowered his hand.

"You okay? You weren't here, for a second."

"Oh." Sophie took a bite of her waffle. "Nothing."

"What?"

He wanted to know.

"I was just thinking," she said. Jake's silence coaxed her to continue. She submitted to the change in their conversation, down a level to dip below the surface. "I saw this video on the news at home. Of a baboon." She shook her head and stared at her plate. "Never mind."

"And the leopard?"

Sophie looked up. "Yes."

"That was wild."

In the viral video, a leopard killed a mother baboon just feet from her nest. Right after, the leopard found the baboon's newborn. The little monkey looked left to right, disoriented. It tried to run away, but the leopard won and carried the baby up a tree in a steep climb. After the leopard lay down, she released the monkey and . . . licked it. Again. And again. The leopard went on to nurture the monkey as if it were its own.

"What about it, though?" Jake asked.

She shrugged. "That there's something about weakness we all respond to. Imperfection, flaws. Across animals."

He smiled—teeth.

"That feels true," he said.

"Anyway," she said. In searching for the next question, she reverted to the one she asked herself most often. "What do you want to do after graduating?"

He laughed.

"What?" she asked.

"Nothing," he said. "It's a great question. I just don't get asked it very often. By people our age, I mean." He leaned back to balance on the rear two legs of his chair. His hands gripped the wooden edge of the table. Tilted precariously, he wondered how much he'd reveal so soon. He pulled himself forward to land. "Do you know who Lionel Padington is?"

"From Padington Associates."

"Right." Lionel had started one of the biggest investment funds in the world, the global Padington Associates, now managing over $50 billion. Lionel himself was worth $4 billion. "I'd like to do something similar."

"Hm." She pushed a square of waffle left, right. "Why?"

Jake had never articulated why out loud. No one had asked, and he'd never volunteered that he wanted to be rich. At best, "I want to be rich" sounded sterile or selfish, and at worst, evil. *"There isn't anyone you couldn't love once you've heard their story,"* Jake's senior-year English teacher had said once. If people knew his, they'd understand.

"Well, what about you?" he dodged. "What do you want to do?"

She took a slow breath.

"I'd like to figure out how the world works. There's so much more here than we know." She pointed in a circle around the room at unnamed, magical invisibilities. Jake pretended to complete her circle and pointed to himself. She laughed. "A lot of people think science is sterile"—Jake's ears pricked up—"and heartless and boring, but not me. I've always had this feeling that there are eyes in everything, that the world is alive down to the atom. But we grow up and start to see things the way we expect. We stop questioning, listening, but I think the universe is always talking to us: through symbols, our guts, or feelings we can't explain. I want to know as much as I can, especially about the big building blocks of reality." Jake pushed his food forward an inch and thoughtfully clasped his hands. "So I study time. I'm sorry. I'm not usually so . . ." She gestured at her mouth.

"I love it," he said, earnest.

She smiled.

"If you could have any dream come true, what would it be?" he asked.

"I'd want to know everything. You?"

"I'd want to have everything."

"What?" she asked as he shrugged.

"There's just a lot of shame around wanting to have."

"I've thought about that, something like that. Whenever I feel weird. When I see there's no one else doing what I'm doing, or making the choices I'm making, I tell myself people are hive creatures, if that makes any sense." Jake shook his head. "So, in a hive, everyone has a role, even if we don't understand it. They all serve a greater purpose. It's not about any bee in particular, even the queen bee. When a queen dies, the hive replaces her. It's all about the hive." Dishes crashed suddenly in the kitchen. Sophie looked up at the wall clock behind Jake: 2:55 p.m. Professor Malchik's office was a ten-minute walk away.

"So—" he began.

"I have to go," she interrupted.

Jake noticed they were the last two in the dining hall. He nodded, stood up. They stacked their trays on metal racks, left, and walked down four flights of stairs to pause at the door leading outside. Their hearts beat faster as each placed a palm flat on the stained-glass pane. Around their hands, silhouettes shifted across burgundy and green. Sophie glanced at the shadows suggesting Frisbee on the quad, but Jake looked singularly at Sophie, his chin angled down, close enough that his breaths warmed her nose.

"What's your phone number?" he asked.

Sophie kissed him. They froze in a wishbone angle joined at the mouth. Jake was following her lead, mirroring her touch and pressure. He waited—interest piqued, hair rising on the back of his neck—for her to budge so he could too. Their lips stayed barely interlocked, exasperatingly surface-deep. Sophie lifted her hand and held one side of his face. His neck was warm, his jawline smooth. She licked his top lip. Jake carefully followed suit. She leaned in to him, and he pulled her body closer, slowly, until she pulled away.

"Can I have your phone?" she asked.

He fished it out of his pocket. She entered her number, handed it back. When they locked eyes, she felt his gaze on her as if she were the only other person alive.

"It was nice to meet you, Jake," she said.

"Sophie."

Jake became so absorbed wording his first text to her—How soon could he see her again? Did she want to study together? Walk anywhere? Get dinner?—that he strayed blocks beyond his dorm, past the Popeyes that cut a soft line between the students and the locals, and into a part of New Haven he'd never seen before.

Peter was sitting alone in his office at 3:29 p.m.

Where was she?

"How can we see time?" the syllabus asked, first page unturned. His composition book underneath was filled with notes from his own reading on prodigies. He flipped through it idly—three thirty now—and happened on the phrase "intellectual companionship." He'd underlined it, figuring Sophie would be starved for it. People her age didn't talk to each other. In one study, nearly 100 percent of millennials said they were better able to express themselves by text than in person. Peter felt like a sociologist reading through research on the "devoicing" epidemic. For Sophie, he'd wondered, who'd been there just to sit and talk? Beyond that, who'd had the intellectual capacity to engage with the full breadth of her mind? To ask about her morning, what she ate for lunch, and then, just as seamlessly, what she thought of the fact that when you line up the angular velocities of planets in their orbits and put them into a ratio, we find what is considered our major and minor musical scales today? Is there a rhythm to the universe? Peter wondered if anyone had ever spoken to her for hours. He flipped the page. Of course, no matter how acquainted he felt with Sophie, they still hadn't met. 3:31 p.m. Had something happened to her? Right as he stood, a knock sounded on his open door.

"Hi, Professor Malchik," Sophie said.

He put his hands in his pockets.

He removed them.

"I'm so sorry I'm late."

She presented as even younger than she already was. The line of midriff between her red tee and shorts was unprecedented in the physics building. He gestured for her to sit and then did the same. Her apology lingered. *It's all right*, Peter wanted to say, but he found himself unable to lie. He flipped almost to the end of his notebook and stopped on the first blank page. He realized he had not shaken her hand. When he'd pictured their meeting, he'd always imagined shaking her hand and saying something prescient, optimistic.

"I expected to start earlier."

"I'm sorry. It won't happen again."

Peter waited for more. She did not speak.

"I was prepared to start at 3 p.m."

"I understand."

"In a course devoted to *time*, a difference of *time* is in fact the most important kind of difference of all."

"I know."

He glanced at the syllabus, listing topics for their session. When he looked up again at Sophie, her head was tilted to the side, a half smile on her lips. In a flash, her smile vanished. She righted her head. Was she distracted? In all his dreams of right now, in all the research he'd done for their semester, he had never imagined delinquency.

"There was a man, Claude Shannon," Peter said suddenly. He massaged his temples. "In 1948, his paper on information theory—it was pivotal, enormous. It outlined the system for what became today's telephones, radio, TV . . . Do you know when he first had that idea?" He looked into Sophie's light blue eyes.

"No."

"Nineteen thirty-nine. Ten years before." Peter tapped the table ten times for emphasis. "Shannon's work during that time wasn't linear, either. The ideas came and went for him throughout those ten years. Progress, then none. Again and again. He had to obsess for a decade." Peter paused to recharge. "I am telling you this, Sophie, to say that genius work takes time. To excel in any one domain, you need to stay committed for years. *Years.*" He paused again. "Today, you were half an hour late. That means your insight will come half an hour later, if at all. I'm sorry to say this, but you are thirty minutes less than what you might have been."

She nodded faintly.

"I won't be late again," she promised.

Peter recognized the fear in her voice. He had a habit of scaring people out of conversations as he focused too much on the meaning of what someone said and not enough on the person speaking. Over the years, Maggie had pointed that out.

Last week, Maggie had invited another couple over for dinner. The woman was an anthropology professor at Yale, though Peter did not catch her name or how Maggie knew them. This professor and her husband—whose name also eluded him—had just returned from a cross-country road trip. She had only just started to describe the vistas of the Columbia River Gorge in Oregon when Peter interrupted to ask how many miles they'd driven in total—*5,360*—and in how much time—*two weeks*—so that was four hundred miles a day, he deduced, and going at sixty miles an hour, almost eight hours a day on the road. Peter fixated on whether they developed backaches from the sedentary position. When the woman showed a video of the gorge, Peter fixated on the telephoto abilities of her iPhone and asked what magnification could she zoom to exactly? How many frames per second? Pixels? His interrogations reached a dead end when one of the couple clammed up, too afraid to invite further scrutiny. At that point, Peter pivoted to extremely literal, mundane lines of discussion, such as, What time did you get up today?

Peter knew he was difficult. His manner could make people feel as though they had drifted empty-headed through life, from one accepted uncertainty to the next. His obsession with the crux of things could be terrifying, but he attributed his faults to caring about the truth. It wasn't that he was insensitive, he thought, it was the opposite. No one else cared as *much* as he did. Other people seemed content to glide unconsciously through life, happily unsure why the stars were the way they were, driven by immediate gratification and five trivial senses. Sophie, he'd hoped, was like him. She wanted to get at the heart of the matter.

He looked at his wall clock, ticking.

"All right," he said. "To the start of time."

CHAPTER 2

Five-year-old Sophie sat on the floor of her family's library and pulled a book off the bottom shelf. The enormous room evoked *Beauty and the Beast*, like a castle corner enchanted into silence and stacked floor-to-ceiling with books. Ladders on metal tracks around the room led up to the top shelves.

Sophie opened the book to a full-page, black-and-white picture of a human skull impaled by a metal rod. The iron pole entered under one cheekbone and exited through the top of the skull. Sophie stared at the details: lipless mouth, long teeth, its empty eye sockets looking back at her. The caption: *Phineas Gage.* Sophie read that, in 1848, a man named Phineas Gage had been working on the railroad when an explosion rocketed a stake through his head. Phineas didn't die immediately. Neither did he suffer debilitating pain, shrinking into more dependent, tortured versions of himself until the end. Instead, right after the accident, Phineas rode by horse to the doctor and lived for another eleven years. The accident didn't affect him physically so much as it changed his personality. Phineas became profane, impulsive, rude, even cruel.

Sophie considered this and, in doing so, gracefully surpassed all expectations for someone so young. Sun warmed tall windows beside her.

"What're you thinking?" her mom, Isabel, asked from the doorway.

"I thought I controlled myself."

Sophie held up the book.

"I see," Isabel said. She walked toward Sophie with dancer-like ease, so fluid, she seemed boneless. When Sophie got older, she'd learn to see her mom's smooth physical style as a special kind of intelligence, as if Isabel's brain filled her whole body and not just the space behind the eyes. Isabel had been a top quant at NASA before she had Sophie in her mid-thirties, left the field, and devoted herself to her family: Ronald, her husband, and Sophie. They had tried to have more children, turning to nonsurgical methods and supplements to help them conceive, but nothing had worked, so Sophie had gotten all of her love.

Isabel sat next to Sophie on the floor and looked tenderly at her daughter. *"Your children are not your children."* The phrase drifted into Isabel's mind from a poem by Kahlil Gibran she'd read while pregnant with Sophie.

Your children are not your children.
They are the sons and daughters of Life's longing for itself.

They come through you but not from you,
And though they are with you yet they belong not to you.

Isabel had read that on the chaise in this library. One of the book-stuffed walls curved into a nook for a red corduroy chaise lounge and leather-top vintage desk with hanging iron handles. Back then, Isabel had thought of course she'd let her daughter go her own way, make her own mistakes—so personal and unique she could copyright them—and learn firsthand the formula for her own happiness. *"Your children are not your children."* It seemed simple. But, sitting next to her, at that moment, she thought Sophie looked just the way she used to—white skin, bright hair, blue fire of curiosity inside, and this deeply harmless kindness, a soft presence that was almost painfully tender. Sophie had never been able to lie. Both Isabel and her daughter were drawn to information, to numbers. As oak tree branches bounced outside the window, equations mapping their curves would have slipped into Isabel's mind with a bit more attention.

"Do you want to go outside?" Isabel asked.

"No, thank you."

Sophie flipped a page. The arched window behind her framed their backyard: meadow-like and colored by small pink flowers, lawn chamomile like dime-size daisies, and wild thyme. Isabel kissed Sophie's head, eyeing the natural playground.

"Do want to go outside *later*?" Isabel asked.

"No, thank you."

Sophie's sweet voice was polite and soft, unintrusive. She flipped another page. Isabel thought her daughter looked so comfortable, so peacefully absorbed in her book, that it would be cruel to tear her away—even though it was a shining April day, and Sophie had been in this library for hours already, picking books off the shelf, reading, and then replacing them precisely. Could Isabel force her daughter to be someone she wasn't?

Sophie finished reading but did not turn the page. She was trying to wrap her head around the fact that people could act so differently after a physical change in the brain. The story had cracked her worldview, sending a fracture through her sense of willing things and feeling an individual essence in herself and others. Didn't she have a soul that glided through everything she did, imbuing it all with Sophieness? Isabel spoke the word *soul* into existence every day. *"Sun is good for your soul." "You have such a beautiful soul, Sophie."* Sophie stared at her own two thumbs on the pages and rubbed them up and down, over the ridgeless edges of words, wondering now how much of the movement she controlled. Meanwhile, Isabel sat beside her, unable to see her daughter's inner world, watching Sophie compute.

On the bus home from kindergarten the next day, Sophie sat in the front row—always counterintuitively the most anonymous one, with plenty of seats—and stared out the window, scanning for home. She didn't talk to anyone as the bus bumped over potholes and made long, theatrical stops. In fact, Sophie hadn't spoken at all that day.

Mom. Isabel waited for Sophie as usual by their mailbox under a jungle of green oaks. Sophie smiled wide, sunnier than the afternoon, itching to stand until the bus stopped and set her free. She darted across the street to hug Isabel hard around the hips. On impact, she forgot all about the loneliness that had plagued her at school. They walked down the driveway until their house came into view: white-shingled, two-story, the windows pure sparkle.

That afternoon, in the library, Sophie read about the brain. Isabel had arranged their two thousand books according to the Dewey decimal system—numbers were an innate preference of hers. Sophie drifted back and forth from Class 100, philosophy and psychology, to Class 500, science, cherry-picking her way through chapters about the mind. It took Sophie a couple of weeks to get through them all, before she turned to the laptop on the desk. Sophie liked that computer: a shining silver compression of infinite books. After school, she started to use it for hours at a time, surfing for answers to her questions. Sometimes Isabel would come in and stand by the nook, watching her daughter scroll down scanned book pages by whipping her fingers up the trackpad. In those moments, when she said, "Sophie," she never got a response. Sophie was absorbed. Isabel would leave unnoticed.

For weeks, Sophie was fascinated by brain tumors: contained areas of brain damage that resulted in predictable personality changes. There was a part of the brain called the fusiform gyrus in the back of the head that was responsible for recognizing faces. If that was harmed, people became unable to identify anyone, even family members. All faces became indistinguishable in a frightening kind of 20/20 blindness. A lump in the frontal lobe, depending on where it grew, could make someone shameless, pedophilic, a compulsive gambler, or unable to make basic choices—like what to wear in the morning, preventing them from getting to work.

Sophie learned her brain *created* her world. She didn't *see* what she *saw*. Her eyes sent incomplete images to her brain, and then her brain filled in the blanks with educated guesses. When her eyes sent disorder, her brain imposed structure. Movies were a prime example of this. Every film was hundreds of thousands of frames in rapid sequence, which the brain blended to suggest movement. Reading about that—the phi phenomenon—prompted Sophie to inform her parents that TV was an illusion. At dinner, over bowls of meaty red spaghetti, Sophie explained the phi phenomenon with surgical exactness. She detailed other illusions, such as pareidolia, the tendency to see meaning where there was only chaos, like faces in a cloud.

Most of people's behavior was automatic. Habit accounted for up to 40 percent of people's choices every day, and those reflexes were stored in the brain. Everything Sophie read was delicious, electric mental sugar, feeding a high. She felt as if she were learning a new language: the wordless way that the world communicated. All she had to do was pay attention. "The universe is full of magical things patiently waiting for our wits to grow sharper," her mom had often quoted the author Eden Phillpotts. Now, Sophie was grasping what that meant. Nature was strange, but knowable. Sophie had always wanted to understand the world, and it appeared the answers were in her brain.

Isabel opened Sophie's first real report card three years later on their library's chaise. The books lining the shelves beside her were fairy tales, section 398.2 in the decimal system. Isabel had a pendant necklace in her jewelry box that read I STILL BELIEVE IN 398.2 in a storybook-like font with spiraling ends. Until then, she had been going through the mail and enjoying the fiery view of changing leaves outside.

She and Ronald had wanted to raise Sophie in a natural place, so they'd settled on Katonah, New York. She tried to get Sophie outside as much as possible. On a family trip to Colorado last year, they'd hiked through the Maroon Bells—godly, sky-high mountains covered with aspen trees—because Isabel had wanted Sophie to meet things bigger than she had ever seen. There was a silencing quality to enormity, which reset the perspective, took her out of the egotistical loop of *I* and *me,* and widened her concerns beyond her next meal, her next weekend, and the protective shell of her routine. The Maroon Bells were magnificent, enormous shoulder blades of earth. The aspens painted them with screen saver–vibrant foliage. Aspens shared roots, and connected ones were considered a single organism, making a grove of aspen trees in nearby Utah the largest organism on planet Earth. They were all connected.

On hikes around Westchester, when she could lure Sophie into them, Isabel pointed out that they were all made of the same stuff: cells converting matter to energy. She wanted Sophie to remember that she was part of nature and to trust her feelings as messengers for the greater order of the universe, from her intuition to her appetite.

Isabel's deference to intuition was radical, boundless. She trusted hers with every question, all the way down to what she should eat. She wanted Sophie to judge for herself, through intimate self-awareness, what foods made her body feel good. If Sophie wanted waffles for dinner, Isabel urged her to eat them with whipped cream piled decadently high, spray-swirled out of the can. Sophie was encouraged to savor warm chocolate cookies straight out of the oven, especially the bittersweet slivers of melted chocolate in there between larger chocolate chunks, the way Isabel made them. Ideally, Sophie would grow up with a healthy sweet tooth and no food anxieties, unlike the other girls in her school who already claimed to be on diets. Isabel wanted Sophie to love food as an extension of herself and to believe that dessert, egg yolks, and the croutons in her salads were all fundamentally okay.

That afternoon, Isabel wore an ankle-length skirt and ballet wrap top that flowered into a bow at the ribs. Her wavy hair was barely tamed in a long side braid. As she opened Sophie's report card, she braced herself. Third grade marked Sophie's first semester with letter grades and comments. Carleton Country Day School's crest stamped the upper right-hand corner, complex enough to pair with the $30,000 price tag. Carleton accepted 15 percent of applicants and attracted the most competitive stay-at-home moms Isabel had ever seen. She imagined they did all their kids' homework and conferred with their husbands about starting early to earn their children spots at Ivy Leagues. She knew women who timed their pregnancies to give birth before Carleton's August 15 cutoff each year.

Isabel scanned the column of A's and flipped to the teachers' comments stapled behind. The first page was written by Sophie's math teacher.

. . . an honor to teach her . . .
. . . a prodigy, as I've already mentioned . . .
. . . exceptionally polite . . .
We'd all benefit from hearing her voice more . . .

Isabel turned the page. The comments from Sophie's other teachers—in English, science, and history—were just as superlative. Everyone singled Sophie out.

Isabel laid the packet on her chest. Of course she had wanted Sophie to be smart. She'd read to Sophie every night since she was born. The words were supposed to bring her mind to life, give her tools to build her own thoughts, and stir her soul with stories of love and adventure. Isabel would sit with Sophie in bed under her skylight, a stamp of changing constellations, and read from the stack of fairy tales on her nightstand. When Sophie was just a year old, though, she repeated the fairy tale from the night before—verbatim. She didn't miss a word, from the opening line of "Beauty and the Beast": *Once upon a time, in a far-off country, there lived a merchant who had been so fortunate in all his undertakings that he was enormously rich* . . . to the end, *And so she did, and the marriage was celebrated the very next day with the utmost splendor, and Beauty and the prince lived happily ever after.* The next night, Sophie recited the fairy tale from the night before. She did the same thing the following night.

Sophie could read by three years old in multiple languages. She taught herself all about the brain, a gateway to her interest in the rest of the body. The previous year, when she was seven, at a dinner party hosted at their home, she'd drawn an ophthalmologist into conversation about "tooth-in-eye" surgery, which entailed that a tooth be removed, a plastic lens inserted, and the whole structure implanted into a patient's cheek, where it grew new blood vessels. The tooth was chosen as a capsule because it was relatively easy to remove and would not be rejected by the body. The lens was then inserted into the eye to restore vision. Sophie asked the ophthalmologist if he had ever performed this surgery—he said he hadn't, something he was barely able to admit given his shock that a child was intimately familiar with a procedure so complex, handling the anatomical terms in her mouth as easily as if they were pink bubble gum.

"How did she learn about this?" he'd asked Isabel.

"Books." Isabel told the truth.

Sophie's teachers had long suggested moving her up in school so that she'd be challenged by her classes. Those nudges began the day Sophie squared a twelve-digit number in her mind toward the end of first grade. Isabel and Ronald refused. They weren't as focused on Sophie's IQ and weren't interested in sending her up to the highest stratum of human computation. Instead, they had their own values and their own lessons to teach Sophie at home.

That afternoon, Isabel waited for Sophie at the top of their driveway. Bright orange oaks looked like fireworks paused at the peak of their explosions. Her cashmere dress swished around her ankles. The school bus came into view and stuttered exhaust as it braked in line with their mailbox. Sophie appeared and skipped across the street, smiling, her French braids whipping every which way. She threw her arms around Isabel in a squeezy, happy hug.

As they walked down the driveway, looking like the same woman separated by three decades, Isabel asked Sophie about school. Did she talk to anyone today? Sophie avoided the question by burrowing her head into Isabel's side. Of course, Sophie didn't like any spotlight on her—which was going to make this discussion about her report card difficult.

"I just want to make sure you aren't taking school too seriously."

"I'm not, Mom."

She gave her daughter a knowing look.

"I just try," Sophie said. "Most people don't try."

"I know."

"I'm supposed to try, right?" Sophie asked.

Isabel nodded.

"School only trains your mind, and that's such a small part of who you are." Isabel squeezed a half-inch of air in front of her. "You're so much more. Your heart and soul, Sophie. We need to nourish the whole you as much as your brain." They walked around the elbow in the driveway. Their house came into view. "I just hope you're making the friends you want. Having fun. Getting outside. The best parts of life come from being connected."

Pavement became gravel.

Prodigy, the report card had said. The trouble, Isabel thought, was the reinforcement. Shiny prizes, praise, and other rewards for intellect could be so intoxicating that they tore prodigies away from other people. Isabel had seen it happen to geniuses at her own high school, at Yale, and at NASA. Their talent for problem-solving brought them attention, and to some, that felt like love. So they threw themselves into their careers, leading more and more solitary lives, and taking on bigger and bigger professional challenges until—on the other side of that breakthrough—there was no one waiting for them to come home. The love they had poured into their work, expecting it to boomerang back, never came.

"I can do better," Sophie said.

"I want you to do worse!" Isabel laughed.

"I'm sorry, Mom."

"Darling," Isabel said. She bent in front of Sophie, suburban wilderness behind her.

"I love you," Sophie said.

The truth of it oozed through her eyes. Sophie was so full of love. When she did venture onto the lawn, it was to leave peeled carrots under juniper bushes for rabbits to eat. She teared up at commercials for the ASPCA. She still hugged Isabel in public. But Isabel was convinced that *giving* love was only half the way to happiness. The other half was to receive it. Sophie could give her love away to books and ideas, but those would never love her back. Sophie would be left with solitary epiphanies and profound insights that few—if any—understood.

"I love you the most. I just want you to be happy." She kissed Sophie's knuckles. "And that starts with talking to other people."

That afternoon, Sophie wandered their lawn where the grass met its hairline of trees. She threw branches into the forest until twilight turned their windows yellow. She knew how her mom wanted her to act. Isabel would've welcomed playdates, birthday parties at the ice rink with delivery pizza, and more hikes together outside. But it was too hard to be around other people. Everyone else was so casual. She felt more. Her insides were so loud. The smaller her world was, the happier she felt, and she was never safer than when she was reading.

Besides, the world desperately wanted to be known.

Sophie thought she'd been on the right track—our *brains* built our world—until this week, when she'd picked up a new book in their library. The tall red cover was thin, a bright scratch on the shelf. Inside, a glossy dinosaur picture filled every two-page spread. Sophie studied the feathered, four-pound microraptors that didn't fly at all. On the next gorgeous spread, a 40,000-ton brontosaurus stood on sand dunes rippled by wind. The sun set over an orange desert by the annotation "Back then, the day was twenty-three hours long." Sophie paused, still standing, her gaze on the final period. She hadn't known a day could be anything but twenty-four hours.

She walked to the laptop, googled, and clicked through blue hyperlinks to *Scientific American*, where she learned Earth didn't rotate at one speed. It was slowing down. The length of one day—the amount of time Earth took to orbit the sun—increased by three milliseconds a century. Sophie sat back, thinking about time, now aware of it passing invisibly by and transforming the morning tick by tick into an afternoon. She leaned forward, into Google, until the next fact that surprised her: until the 1800s, every town in America had its own time zone. This wasn't a problem until railroads connected people from different ones, leading the country to adopt standardized time zones in 1883. Sophie checked the clock on her laptop: 11:23 a.m.—deceptively steady, but those numbers weren't steady at all. Time wasn't absolute.

Sophie lobbed another branch into the dark forest. It was too deep into fall to smell much of the grass, mossy bark, or dry leaves under her sneakers. Back at her house, the kitchen windows were bright, as if the last foliage had moved inside. Isabel, light on her feet, was taking a stack of three plates out of the cupboard. Would her mom be sad if she read more tonight? She'd spent time outside. Besides, she had a hunch now: she'd thought the brain *created* the world, but now, she saw space and time as master controllers of the universe.

In the kitchen, Isabel moved a crusty round of sourdough from oven to table in the toasty air. Ronald would be home soon. She checked on Sophie fifty yards away, still clearing sticks. Sophie had been pacing the same line for over an hour, back and forth, with such repetition that she must've been deep in thought. It didn't look like fun. The yard was too dark. Sophie was too alone. Maybe Isabel had been too harsh that afternoon. Maybe she shouldn't force Sophie outside so often. After all, no matter where Sophie was, she was always in her own head.

Isabel sat at the head of the table between Ronald and Sophie, watching her daughter cut a chicken breast into diamonds. Wax thickened the bottoms of their candlesticks. Ronald lifted a forkful of pumpkin lasagna, thinning a string of mozzarella up to his mouth. Sophie was describing her latest book, a biography of Albert Einstein. She explained that Einstein had been handling patents having to do with coordinating clocks across railway stations in Switzerland when he'd come up with his famous theory of relativity.

"People were trying to make clocks match," Sophie said.

"When did you read all this?" Isabel asked.

"Lunch."

Ronald swallowed.

"You read all during lunch?" Isabel asked.

Sophie nodded.

Isabel and her husband exchanged glances.

"It was barbecue day outside."

Isabel imagined Sophie reading the three-inch-thick biography of Einstein—she knew the exact edition from their library—alone at one of the picnic tables by Carleton's soccer field. Sophie resumed sculpting her lemon rosemary chicken. Each diamond was a perfect replica of the one before, straight-edged and bite-size.

"Did you know there's a planet made of diamonds?" Sophie asked.

Isabel's face was tender.

"Where's that, sweetie?"

"Four thousand light-years away."

Sophie etched another diamond.

"It's only a little bigger than Jupiter, but it's twenty times as dense."

Was it really the right choice, holding Sophie back? Her daughter loved to think. Isabel imagined Sophie taking the SATs in a gym full of high school seniors twice her size, hopping from one ellipse to the next, shading each with inside-the-lines care.

Sophie laid her knife and fork at four o'clock.

"Meet you in your room?" Isabel asked.

Sophie stood up.

"You know who's the best?" she asked. Isabel smiled, recognizing her daughter's end-of-dinner routine. Sophie kissed her mom three smacky times on the cheek, then walked to her dad, hugged him around the neck, and kissed him the same.

"You are!" Ronald said.

"No, *you.*" Sophie turned to Isabel. "And *you.*"

Sophie put her clean plate in the dishwasher before prancing upstairs. Isabel and Ronald swallowed their final bites and then tidied the kitchen, dividing cleanup down the middle. Once done, Ronald stood behind Isabel and massaged the slopes between her shoulders and neck.

"Love you," he said.

She turned around. They kissed.

"Love you."

As they walked upstairs, Ronald kept one hand on Isabel's shoulder. He was an inch shorter than she, balding slightly, and by all accounts a reliable, predictable man. He'd worked at Pfizer since graduating from Williams. At his twentieth college reunion last year, he'd spent most of the time talking to Isabel. They'd gotten cheese slices in Williamstown before driving home ahead of the main "Dinner Buffet, Dancing, and Surprise" event to beat the traffic. He'd fallen in love with Isabel for her luminous mind, matched by a depth of heart, and she made him feel interesting. He saw their relationship and magical daughter as the proudest accomplishments of his life. They parted left and right at the top of the stairs.

Knock. Knock.

"Come in!"

Sophie was already in bed, smiling. Isabel sat next to Sophie, their backs to the plush yellow headboard studded with fabric buttons. The books on Sophie's nightstand were stamped with Carleton Library stickers on the spines. Isabel scanned the titles: all mentioned time travel except for the one on Einstein and *The Secret Life of Salvador Dalí*, a biography of the surrealist famous for painting melting clocks. Sophie reached over Isabel to tug her floor lamp's string, clicking the room into darkness. The skylight framed a dazzling patch of stars. This area gave some of the best views that Isabel had ever seen, and she had visited observatories in Europe—at high altitudes with premium telescopes—as a special guest.

Here, Isabel had spent years teaching Sophie about the constellations above them. Just yesterday, she'd pointed up and explained that the colors of stars ranged from red to white to blue depending on their temperature. Red was the coolest color, white was warmer, and blue was the hottest, at over 12,000 Kelvin. She finished the night by quoting some Oscar Wilde, reciting from memory, "Nothing can cure the soul but the senses, just as nothing can cure the senses but the soul," which she thought were gorgeous words urging people to trust themselves and value the body's intelligence. We were as natural as the stars. Tonight, as usual, she drew from the day in choosing a lesson. She searched the back of her mind for something about connection.

"Do you know what supersymmetry is?" Isabel asked.

Sophie shook her head.

"It's the idea that every particle has a partner," Isabel said. "Particles, as you know, are the smallest bits of the universe. Supersymmetry says that every particle has its own 'superpartner,' as they're called, even though none of these have been observed." She stroked Sophie's warm head. "There's still so much we don't understand. Our best theories about how everything works would predict that particles don't have mass." She paused for emphasis. "But obviously, this isn't true. You look around and see everything has mass. You. Me. Adding superpartners to some important equations gives us results that match what we actually see . . ."

Slowly, Sophie stopped moving.

"I've always liked that idea. That there's a partner out there for every particle. Something mystical and strange, or someone . . ." Isabel remembered the weight of Ronald's hands on her shoulders. She fell silent when she heard Sophie's breaths heavy with sleep. She gazed at her daughter. Sophie's hair spiraled around her head like galaxy arms around a central eye. She hoped Sophie felt how completely she was loved, even when there was no one around to say it. She kissed Sophie's forehead before she disappeared.

CHAPTER 3

Jake halted in the lobby before the glass door: a homeless man was poking his forearm with a needle. Out of the doorman's line of sight, he jabbed the syringe in and out, stabbing for a vein. His cargo pants billowed. Wind blew his long sleeve onto his chest like an X-ray tracing his bones. His hair was just as dark as Jake's—Jake recognized his dad.

Rather, a version of him. But unmistakable.

Thinner, wrinkled, frustrated.

Still, Dad.

Jake stood immobile in shiny brown loafers, a two-button blazer, and a navy tie with red stripes, his uniform for the first day of eighth grade. The key chain on his backpack—a stainless-steel tag printed with TRINITY, his school's name—swung in smaller and smaller arcs until it hung still. He had not seen his dad, Tom Kristopher, in five years. Now, here they were, close enough to have a conversation. Behind him, grown-ups in

Barbour jackets and oxford shirts speed-walked to work, obey-ing the unspoken norm to ignore the homeless on New York City streets. Dad dropped the needle and wandered out of view.

Jake was too shocked to move.

His heartbeat pumped his throat.

"You okay?" Lucas, the doorman, asked.

The last time Jake had seen his father was in their old apart-ment in Harlem, leaving to disappear for the weekend like he always did after payday. Jake had reimagined that moment so many times—feeling the delicate memory for all of its details—that he was no longer sure what the exact circumstances had been. Jake had handled the image of his dad's broad back reced-ing in the doorframe too much to trust it anymore.

Since then, Jake's mom, Janice, had married again, this time to George Hershaw III. Something about George—never "Dad"—always felt off. He was so much older. She didn't act in love with him. When the three of them strolled around Tribeca—from Hermès to Gucci, "treating" Mom, as George put it—and George leaned in to kiss her, she usually offered just her cheek. When George reached for her hand, she sometimes held her own instead. She ordered a kale salad without dressing when he was around, but split a large pizza and garlic knots with Jake when George was away on business.

Mom was beautiful—lustrous hair, dense eyebrows, a natural tan—and that seemed to be what George liked best about her. All of his nicknames came from her looks: Dollie, Dimples, Caramel. She'd always been thin, but when she'd started dating

George, her body had changed. Her biceps rounded. Her thighs hardened. She grew squares of abs.

Her courtship with George was fast and glitzy, and had ended last summer in a Montauk wedding that he'd paid for from save-the-date to sparkler send-off. Janice, thirty-two, took George, fifty-two, with no children of his own, to be her lawfully wedded husband. Jake didn't eat much that night. He didn't even taste the four-tiered, three-layer wedding cake that stacked lemon sponge on raspberry sponge on red velvet foundation. His mom tried to dance with him, and Jake made an effort, but the band George had flown in from Atlanta was too loud; the tent at Gurney's Montauk Resort was packed full of strangers; and George had been pawing his mom in ways that turned his stomach. Big hairy hands all over a white wedding dress felt wrong.

"Jake, you okay?" Lucas pressed.

"I'm fine. See you later, Lucas."

The sidewalks were crowded.

Needle abandoned.

Mom did love Dad, though. They had grown up together in a Catholic town on Long Island, dated in secret starting in fifth grade, and made the seismically unpopular choice to have him when they were nineteen. Instead of going to college, when Mom was seven months pregnant, they'd left for jobs in New York City without anyone's blessing. The way they explained it to Jake: they chose each other over everyone else. "When you find out who your family is, that's all that matters," Dad said once while looking at Mom.

Their first apartment was decked out with CVS-printed photos of them: snapshots from their city hall wedding in four-by-four layouts, each box a kiss from a different angle, their ear-to-ear joy brighter than the glossy photo finish; and then, pictures from a road trip through Maine, the two of them kissing under lighthouses by rocky coastlines, infant Jake strapped to Mom's chest; and then, the three of them cheers-ing red-and-yellow-streaked hot dogs at a Mets game. Their home in Harlem was a shrine to their family, lacking every luxury except love.

Dad's first job had been in sales at Booyah Sports, talking up hiking gear to those with wanderlust. Mom had waitressed at an Italian restaurant on the Upper East Side. They were happy. It shone through Mom's face when Dad came home at night. They liked to kiss new parts of each other, so Dad would always plant one on Mom in an amusingly bizarre place—under her chin, behind her ear—and she'd return the strangeness by kissing his wrists or Adam's apple.

The recession took their jobs without warning. Gifts at home became necessities: shampoo and conditioner on birthdays. Joy gave way to focus. Mom and Dad started to bicker, tension rising slow as water coming to a boil, mostly around "asking for help." Mom got hired first at the Glen Oaks Club, where she waited on serene members in tennis whites. That alone was not enough. They moved to a smaller apartment but kept all their photos, even though the frames crowded the kitchen counter and foggy glass shelf over the bathroom sink.

Mom took a second job at a dry cleaner. Meanwhile, Dad wouldn't take a job paying less than he used to make. When his application for vice president of business development at Home Depot was rejected—a job that required a college degree— Mom yelled so precisely, Jake learned how searingly articulate someone could be with tears streaming down her face. She broke three picture frames that night by slamming them against the floor. Dad stared at the glass shards from his seat on their slanted sofa and calmly agreed to change.

He accepted a job in construction: a graveyard shift in Manhattan four nights a week. On his nights off, he started to go out drinking with "the boys" on his shift. Months passed. Dad stayed out later, sometimes not coming home until Jake was leaving for school. The two of them would pass each other in the stairwell between walls of chipping gray paint. Dad started to disappear the day after he got paid; then for entire weekends; and then for five whole years.

Until today.

After school, Jake stepped off the subway a few stops early on Fourteenth Street instead of going all the way home to Tribeca. Misty rain wet his face. Each breath nipped melting clouds. He wandered over dark sidewalk into Mah-Ze-Dahr, where he ordered a slice of carrot cake. Everything else—cheesecake with black graham cracker crust, sugar-dusted brioche doughnuts, cream-filled choux pastries—had been pillaged, but the carrot cake needed love. He took George's Chase Sapphire card out of his wallet and swiped it limply.

Jake ate his slice with a plastic fork on a skinny counter lined with outlets. On his phone, he read a *New York Times* article about an opioid crisis in the United States and studied a list of slang names for drugs—Apple Jacks? Black Pearl? Junk?—on AddictionCenter.com that did not elucidate much. Jake had never done drugs. He hung in his nook, unseen, until the windows were bruisy and he felt compelled to leave. Mom would worry soon.

As he walked home, he searched everyone sitting on the sidewalk for his own eyes, his own hair, his own genes. The air was rainy. His lips felt cold. A cardboard bed lay flat in front of Starbucks, ominously missing its occupant. George didn't like Starbucks. He refused to pay for any coffee there, saying it wasn't a coffee bar, it was a chain of public restrooms. Jake's blood thumped louder the closer he got to home, but he didn't pass anyone he knew. When he stepped back through the lobby's glass door—no needle—he figured Dad had moved on. There was no way Dad knew where they lived, anyway.

"Good evening, Jake," Ed, a night doorman, said.

"Sir."

Elevator.

Ninth floor.

Jake turned his key. The long hallway peeked into their bright kitchen, where Mom sat on a stool, her arms crossed over her chest.

"Love you," George said.

"Thank you," Janice said icily.

"Say you love me."

"I love you." Her voice was flat.

"Look at me and say it."

"Hello?" Jake announced himself. The fact that Mom and George were at odds didn't surprise him. George loved her "moods," as he called them, writing off whatever reasonable qualms she had with him as irrational, emotional swings.

Mom stood up. She wore black yoga leggings and a clingy sweatshirt that hugged her sculpted waist. Her hair shone in a sleek line from her high ponytail to her mid-back. Jake set his damp backpack in the hallway and hung his rain jacket on the coat rack, which looked like a tree skeleton leafed with Barbour, Moncler, and Patagonia fleeces. He slipped his New Balance sneakers off heel by heel and walked across the white shag rug into the kitchen. George was leaning against the counter and eating dime-size gluten-free chocolate chip cookies straight from the bag. His belly rounded his white-and-blue-striped polo.

"Where were you?" Mom asked.

"Around."

She looked concerned.

"Chasing tail?" George asked.

"George, please."

Mom blushed. He chuckled devilishly.

"Do you want tea?" she asked.

Jake nodded. He was too stuffed to want anything more inside him, but he rarely told her no. On the stool she left vacant, he slumped and stared at the sink where Mom was filling a cherry-red Le Creuset kettle. She set it on the stove and swept blue fire under its seat. George had given Mom carte blanche to remodel anything she didn't like about the apartment when they moved in, but nothing had needed an upgrade. Their modern three-bedroom in the heart of Tribeca, with floor-to-ceiling views of the Hudson River, was like their wedding had been—lacking only one immaterial thing. George tossed another handful of cookies into his mouth.

"I'm spent," he announced as he left the room.

Alone with Jake, Mom sealed the bag with a plastic butterfly clip and returned it to the cabinet over the stove. Every step delineated her quads.

"You gonna tell me where you really were?" she asked quietly.

"I saw Dad."

She froze.

"Outside. This morning. He was jabbing himself." Jake mirrored the stabbing motion he'd seen his father make toward his forearm. "By our building."

She gripped the sink with both hands.

"We didn't talk," Jake said. "He left."

"For where?"

"I don't know."

Mom leaned forward; under the chandelier, her face looked worn. Bags shaded a second strip of eyeliner under her eyes. Up close, her pain was stronger than her mask.

"I'm sorry," he said.

"It's not your fault."

The teakettle's scream startled Mom into filling two steaming mugs. She dropped a chamomile bag into each one and sat beside him. Neither spoke. Jake reached for her hand. As his fingers curled around hers, he wished he could hold her pain for her, too.

George lost his job at the mutual fund when Jake started high school. There was no talk of his getting a new one. The prospect of working so hard again so soon did not excite him. Instead, he entertained ideas such as investing his savings in a tennis-related startup; fundraising for a new designer surfboard company that would hold board meetings in Hawaii; or moving to Argentina and retiring. If George did move, of course they'd follow. He was their patriarch and owner. If he wanted to move to the Andes and ranch, then all three of their lives would be uprooted. It suddenly didn't matter that they lived in a spacious Tribeca apartment filled with modern art. Jake felt alarmingly dependent on an unreliable man.

Jake got his own part-time job helping rich kids with their homework. He was charming enough to earn good cash tips from their moms and saved everything he could. Despite his new gig, Jake had never spent less. He stopped taking taxis. When he needed to *buy* food, he got it from CVS, where, in the refrigerated area, they sold yogurts for twenty cents cheaper per container than Duane Reade. Jake had always gotten good grades, but now he scored the best in his class. He wanted to work at Lionel Padington's firm on Wall Street, which paid the highest salaries and only hired Ivy League grads with 4.0s. He was focused on going to Yale, which he perceived as the less stuck-up Harvard. He read SAT prep books as if they were maps showing the path out of jail.

Jake's junior fall, he opened the door to find their hallway full of suitcases. The black Tumi bags were stuffed like popped popcorn, corners unzipped and bursting with Mom's cashmere. Mom's shoes filled three paper bags on the floor. The fourth had a Yale sweatshirt on top, which she'd bought on their college tour the prior week.

Jake had just returned from Essen, a no-frills restaurant catering to office types. Jake ate dinner there a few nights a week. He liked their prices—a heaping to-go Styrofoam container of vegetables and hard-boiled eggs for less than $10—and the fact he could work there uninterrupted. He read alone next to his food in the upstairs area filled with dinky tables and steel chairs. It teemed with business casual sorts on efficient breaks, a crowd that resonated with his sense of purpose. The only drawback was that the upstairs had no windows, offering no clue as to passing time. It was later now than he'd wanted to get home, 10 p.m. on Friday.

"You went in there because you wanted to find something!" George's voice was distorted by shouting.

Jake froze, still in khakis and a school tie.

"Don't . . . blame . . . me," Mom said.

The spaces between her words were wet.

"No man's clean! Not fucking one."

Jake walked in slow motion. He passed an overturned stool in the kitchen. He waited outside their door, sour-stomached.

"You're disgusting," Mom snapped.

"You wanted to catch me."

Jake imagined what might have happened. The door swung open to reveal Mom's red stare. She pulled Jake in for a hug that he was too shocked to reciprocate. Her eyes bled tears onto his oxford. George looked sweatier than usual in a country club polo.

"What the fuck're you looking at?" George demanded.

Mom swung around.

"We're leaving," she announced.

"You'll be back."

Mom led Jake into his own room.

"Can you pack?" she managed.

"What's going on?"

Mom shut the door and sat on his bed, her forehead on her wrists.

"I didn't think it'd get to me. Didn't know it'd be this bad." She shook her head slowly, clearly at an internal slideshow. "This isn't the right place for you to be . . ." She looked at Jake through glassy eyes. "I'm so sorry."

"Mom, it's okay."

"His phone . . . So many."

She covered her eyes.

"I'm so sorry," she said.

They hugged.

"I'll help you pack."

"Where will we go?" he asked.

Mom was in no state to help. He pulled his own Tumi from under the bed and began filling it: pressed khakis in beige and navy, a blazer, a foot-tall stack of workout shirts, running shorts, boxers, and handfuls of white athletic socks with check marks on the ankle. He didn't know what to bring. He grabbed blindly.

"A hotel. I booked a room for tonight." She shook her head. "I just kept thinking, what if you'd been here when he brought one of them home? I'm so sorry." She covered her eyes. "I'll work again. I have my own savings. An account we never merged."

"Me too."

Jake had already invested his tutoring money in the most re-liable companies he could find. He wasn't betting on risky new technologies. He only trusted businesses with proven strategies. The power of time—the greatest multiplier of all—would yield the most enormous gains. All he had to do was wait for his sum to grow. So far, he had $19,012.

"We're going to be fine," she said.

"I know."

"We're going to be fine."

*　　　*　　　*

A week later, they moved to Harlem. Their new apartment was the same size as their old one ten blocks south, both skirting seven hundred square feet; the former tenant had left his sofa for free, and they each had their own skinny bedroom. They shared a bathroom, but it was more than Jake had expected. After all, Mom had signed an iron-clad prenup with George. None of his credit cards had worked since they left. $17,021. Jake had withdrawn money to help while Mom waited to hear back from the country clubs where she was interviewing.

For dinner their first night at home, Mom bought KFC. Over the cooling food, they talked about the future. That was a happier place. Early applications to Yale were due in one year. Meanwhile, Mom ate exactly half of their shared green beans side and half of the mac and cheese from the $5 Fill-Up menu, which came with chicken nuggets mixed in like meaty pasta croutons. Her smile looked strenuous. $17,021.

Jake headed home with his $12 Old Navy scarf over his nose and mouth, $10 beanie pulled down to his eyebrows, exposing just his stare to the cold. Snow flurries wet dark air, lit a little in the yellow shadows of Harlem's street lamps. He was imagining what Mom might have made for dinner. They ate together every Monday, the one night of the week she got home first. Her chicken stir-fry was his favorite, chili a close second. Food and the future were his two mental Band-Aids, good for mending painful moments.

After they left George, Jake's junior year became a long stretch of routines. He worked out every morning, turned in early every night, and tutored twenty hours a week. Mom returned to waitressing at Glen Oaks and took a waxing job at Exhale Spa on the Upper East Side. They enjoyed small luxuries, like movies in the theater, herbed popcorn from trucks in Central Park, and home-cooked meals on Mondays. Mom stopped drinking—not that she ever had much—which Jake guessed was in part to spare the expense and in part a reflection of the new atmosphere at home. There was an unspoken sense of being joined in the same endeavor: getting Jake on the best track. Both were solemnly devoted to it. Jake didn't decorate his room except for printed sheets of Yale's courses taped to his wall. He grew his portfolio. $21,031.

Now, in mid-December, Jake was waiting for Yale's decision on his early application. They never mentioned George, though Jake deduced major developments: he and Mom were officially divorced. George would pay Jake's remaining tuition at Trinity, but no more. He wasn't interested in keeping up with their lives.

A block from home, Jake saw their building's door ajar. A spray of snow through the entryway left it white and watery. He clenched his jaw. He hated that, the insecurity of it. Their own home. He shut the door, angry, and jumped upstairs two at a time to find the door open to their apartment, too. Lights on. Jake pushed the door open, slammed it shut, and strode into the kitchen, boots on, to find Mom sitting at the kitchen table with her hands wrapped around a chipped mug of hot water. She still wore her Glen Oaks uniform, its green collar visible under her parka. A thick envelope waited on the table with a bulldog stamped on front. Mom started to cry. A thick envelope. He tore it open.

Congratulations . . . .

He swung from word to word.

Full scholarship . . .

Mom cried harder. He hugged her in her chair—exuberant, ecstatic, relieved—until she started laughing. They jumped up and down together in a moment ridiculously youthful and summer bright. The future was almost here.

CHAPTER 4

Hours after they met, Jake and Sophie ventured into Bass, the underground library at Yale. His first text had invited her to study. Now, they passed leather chairs, marble tables, and bookcases arranged with the symmetrical precision of a royal garden, all the way to a study room meant for a small group. As Sophie unzipped her backpack, she imagined how their elbows might graze if she got lost in her own mind, forgot her body. She was on edge from proximity to him. It amplified the silence and magnified every detail.

So close to Sophie, Jake noticed that she didn't smell like anything: unscented, just plain clean. The girls he was used to at Trinity had started making themselves up in middle school. They ironed their hair until it gave off a whiff of burnt plastic; glossed their lips with tubes of Lip Venom, supposedly plumping them; hid their faces under bronzers; and doused themselves with so much perfume that classrooms smelled like the ground floor of Bloomingdale's. Jake found Sophie's naturalness new and sensual. It had the quality of being undressed. Jake cleared his throat and opened his laptop, $1,199 from the Apple store on Fifth Avenue. He opened his usual set of tabs: *Wall Street Journal, New York Times,* and *Barron's.* He kept a Google doc open—named "Future"—where he wrote his ideas on where the world was going.

Sophie uncapped a Bic pen over her problem set from Professor Malchik and leaked her mind into neat blue print. She etched Σs and ∫s.

They relaxed into the silence.

Sophie resurfaced after an hour: 7:32 p.m. She put her pen down—first problem solved—and looked up to find Jake in his own focus cocoon. He was so singularly absorbed, she had the strange feeling she was staring at herself in her library at home. There was passion in his focus. Being so close to him *now,* in this unselfconscious state, felt intimate. What was happening between them? This ease, so soon after they'd met. She sank back into her problem set.

Jake waved his hand between them.

She checked her watch: 8:16 p.m.

"Sorry," she admitted.

"It was cute."

She covered her face.

"I was just—"

"Thinking."

She smiled.

"Happens to me, too," he said.

"We disappear."

He smiled. She made it seem like magic.

"Do you want anything from the café?" he asked. Bass Café upstairs had a small counter stocked with pastries and refrigerated to-go items.

"Oh! Sure."

"My treat. What's your drink?"

"Milkshake."

Jake chuckled.

"What?" she asked.

Her eagerness had reminded Jake of being very young: falling asleep in restaurants, the word *grown-ups*, and the illicit allure of sugar.

"What flavor?"

"Oreo?"

Jake smiled. He stood up.

"Be right back."

Jake stood in line at Bass Café behind four girls with swinging ponytails. They chatted—about Franzia, a Mike Posner concert, being gluten-free, and a "stoplight party" where green means go and red is you're taken—each topic with an infinitesimal half-life. Their lukewarm interest in each subject was never hot enough to spark a lasting fire. He looked over his shoulder toward Bass, thinking about her.

Then, his turn.

"Five fifty," the cashier demanded.

When he paid for Sophie's milkshake, Jake realized they were on a date. Their time together had felt natural, but that's exactly what this was—a first date. He'd had the sense that dating was supposed to be more done up: more showing off, bright plumage, chest puffing, nervous energy, and self-doubt. But every moment with Sophie was calm. A date where two people did what they would've done alone—hopefully she saw the intimacy in that? They weren't leaning into idealized versions of themselves. It was just them.

With their drinks—her large Oreo milkshake, his free cup of tap water—he walked back through the turnstile. Individual study rooms lined either side of him. In one, a boy in glasses shucked a Crunchy Peanut Butter CLIF Bar, its crinkle silent. Jake loved the quiet here, shrine-like. Sophie apparently did, too. He'd never met anyone else who . . . "disappeared"? Sophie was deep in thought when he reached their room and opened the door with his elbow. She jolted, then stood, took the Styrofoam cup, and admired all sixteen ounces topped with a whimsical swirl of whipped cream and black Oreo crumbs.

"Thank you!"

Sophie took a sip.

"What've you been working on?" he asked.

"The start of time." She was solving the first Friedmann

equation, which described the trajectory of the universe. "This calculates how much the universe is expanding or contracting. And when our world will ultimately come to an end. You just have to input how much matter, energy, and radiation exists, and when time began."

"Time had a start?"

She nodded.

"Thirteen point eight billion years ago."

"Huh."

"If time had been around forever, the sky would have infinite stars, right?"

Jake tried to imagine that: the night sky bright as day, stars like carpet.

"What was before that?" he asked.

"Before the big bang? No one knows. *After*, there were a few hundred million years of darkness before any stars were born." She reflected. "Maybe, though, when we see time, we'll have a better idea what was before."

"I like your confidence," Jake blurted.

Sophie blushed, happy.

"Sorry. I just meant not everyone has a direction."

"Thank you."

"What do you think time looks like?"

She tilted her head to the side. Visualizing time *was* tricky. Doing so challenged the paradigm that people could only infer time by observing other things. She imagined people in previous eras had struggled with the idea of a round Earth in the same way, because it defied everyone's feeling that the ground was flat. Sophie's hunch was that if she gained a better understanding of time, she'd understand where to look for it. Maybe it was joined with matter at the subatomic level in ways people couldn't naturally detect.

"I don't know. Yet."

She smiled.

"You gonna build a telescope? A time telescope?"

"Maybe I will."

The silence was stuffed full of loud thoughts, tension.

"Well, if—*when* you see time, will you show me?"

Sophie, warmer, nodded.

"The library will close in five minutes."

Jake and Sophie exited, climbing stone stairs outside. On Cross Campus—the quad fenced by Sterling Library and Gothic dorms called "colleges"—stragglers headed home. Jake and Sophie were the only pair on the lawn. They stopped under the starry sky: glowy, pointillistic. Jake tried to look up through Sophie's eyes. She saw such details, so naturally zoomed in. In the gorgeous spray above, Jake noticed that not all stars were the same size. Bigger dots interrupted dusty patches. He projected shapes between them: a smile arc, a pair of eyes. He realized that not all stars glowed the same, either. Some were brighter, others more gently gorgeous. *Star* was one word, but there was breadth to the lights.

"Do you want to study tomorrow?" Jake asked.

"Yes, please."

He smiled.

"I'm Hopper," she added quickly.

She pointed to the college closest to them. Jake realized they hadn't asked each other the most common question at Yale. *What college are you in?* All freshmen were sorted into one. Affiliation lasted for life. Each was a gated community with its own dining hall, common area—a clubby, paneled room usually with a piano—gym, and library, and sometimes a basketball court or theater underground.

"I'm Berkeley," he said.

He pointed to the college next to hers.

She laughed.

"We forget anything else?" he asked.

"Right past the basics."

"What's your sign?"

"Gemini. You?"

"Sagittarius. Okay, all caught up now."

He walked her to Hopper's iron gate, where they stood under a streetlamp, the yellow windows of her college, and 13.8 billion years of starlight. He leaned in to kiss her and in the same second she wrapped her arms around his neck. They held each other, frozen in the warmest way. Sophie felt all of the passion that had been driving his focus in Bass this time directed at her.

"Night, Jake."

"Sophie."

As Jake walked back to Berkeley, he looked up at the stars he wouldn't have noticed without her. He thought there was a sparkling crystal quality to them. It was as though he were looking at champagne in a flute—if those bubbles were frozen in time.

Jake and Sophie studied together every night for the next few weeks. During this time, he learned her tendency to ask dreamy questions usually orbiting youthful concerns. She asked him, *"What was your favorite birthday?"* He couldn't remember the last time he'd celebrated his. Then, *"If you were an animal, what would you be?"* He chose an eagle without thinking. And then, *"What's your favorite kind of doughnut?"* Apple cider, he guessed. Meanwhile, Jake wondered if Sophie had ever had any adult experiences. It entranced him how her genius IQ was paired with interests so stunningly young—down to her sweet tooth. On study breaks, he witnessed her eat six-inch snickerdoodles double-dusted with cinnamon sugar, caramel stroopwafels dipped in apple juice, and even sugar out of the packet.

"What was your *favorite birthday?"* He returned that question to learn Sophie had never had a birthday party. He found that strange for someone so attractive. Didn't beautiful girls always have friends? *"If you were an animal, what would you be?"* An eagle, she answered after him. *"What's your favorite kind of doughnut?"* Rock candy, she claimed, and then described a pink one sprinkled with candy shards. Unlike Sophie, Jake added more serious questions that were grounded in reality. *"Who's*

your best friend?" My mom, she said. *"What's your biggest fear?"* Being in a crowd in a place I don't know—something Jake admitted sounded pretty horrifying. *"What do you believe that no one else does?"* One day, we will see time.

"Do you want to come over?" Jake asked late that fall.

Beyond their glass wall, students at the communal table were stuffing their backpacks. Arms threaded Barbour sleeves. A group in Yale Bulldogs sweatshirts passed.

Jake's latest question electrified the air.

Sophie looked down at her problem set, the last page blank under the final prompt, and flipped it over. She smiled yes. As they packed their backpacks, she felt her heart beat, her breath whoosh. Her sense of her own body was piqued. Right before the turnstiles, they stopped for the bag check. A suited guard zigzagged a flashlight over hardcovers, her spiral notebook, and a pack of sparkling gel pens. Then it lasered inside Jake's over a trash bag of gym clothes, his neon sneakers, and his laptop tucked into the back inner pocket.

"Thank you, sir," Jake said.

Sophie smiled. *Sir.* She loved his grave respect for others. *Sir.* That was how he ordered at Bass Café, Ashley's Ice Cream, and Insomnia Cookies, too. He spoke with such formality to strangers, with such purpose, it was as if he thought the universe would pivot depending on his word choice. He carried himself with the same intention.

They climbed the stairs to Cross Campus.

"Sorry, your question," he said.

"Superpower?"

He nodded. Jake had been about to answer Sophie's question, *"If you could have any superpower, what would it be?"* when the loudspeaker made its closing announcement and he pivoted wildly to invite her over. They were now walking to Berkeley over craggy stones jigsawed together, saving the grass from their sneakers. He reached for her hand and held it loosely, their fingers linked without pressure at the points of connection.

"I think about focus a lot," he said. "Some people can just concentrate. No matter where they are, or how chaotic it is, they can fixate on the thing of their choice. There's a lot of talk about ADHD, but I think I have the opposite. I can focus on one thing, just devote myself, for such a long time, it has to be . . . not a superpower, but something that makes me feel different. When I'm like that, there's only one thing on my mind, and the rest just—"

"Superfocus?" Sophie said.

"Ha, sure. And I think you have it, too." He squeezed her hand. "I know that doesn't answer your question, though. If I had to have a superpower, maybe . . ." He remembered their first lunch. "I'd help you know everything."

A week after they'd met, he'd brought her a gift: *Physics of the Impossible,* a book by Michio Kaku. He'd bought it at the Yale Bookstore, wrapped it himself, and taped a bag of Skittles on top next to a stick-on bow. *"You definitely know all this already,"* he said as she opened it in Bass. *"It's more so you have something from me in your room."* The sexuality of it shocked him as soon as the words left his mouth. Sophie just smiled, unembarrassed, as if she had no idea what illicit activities might unfold in her room between them.

Tonight, Jake had asked her over only because he wanted to keep talking. Sophie was an exceptional listener. Her attention was palpable, generous. She gave their conversations the same care she gave her work. Jake found it entrancing to watch her solve equations every night, to think that the universe was in her scribbling, that reality was so easily at her fingertips. He'd just wanted more of her time, maybe to ask *"If you could have any superpower . . ."* in return, but the closer they got to his room, the more he imagined how they could move together. He buzzed them into Berkeley's courtyard and pictured kissing her, pressing her against the white plaster wall of his single. He guided Sophie to his entryway.

"How're your roommates?" Sophie asked.

"Not sure."

Jake shared a common room with three others he barely saw. They climbed the stairs.

Sophie huffed. She was acutely aware of her body now: the pipe of her throat as she swallowed, the fleshy tops of her thighs against the inseam of her jeans, the button snap on her belly. She wasn't used to this: her body. She'd met with a psychiatrist only once, at her mom's request in middle school. During that meeting, Dr. Putnam had asked, *"Do you think you live in your head?"* Back then, Sophie had thought, *Of course. My world is created in my head, and your world is created in yours.* But it didn't feel like the full answer. Since then, Dr. Putnam's question had drifted back into her mind, unsolved. Now, Sophie understood what he'd meant. *This* was being out of her head. She was living in her whole body, so close to Jake on the way to his place. This was not analysis. This was the thick of it, pure feeling.

Jake unlocked the door to his common room, giving way to a wide-screen TV, ragged futon dusted with stiff potato chip crumbs, faded blue rug, lacrosse sticks leaning against the wall, tennis racquets—a claustrophobic amount of things.

"Which one's yours?" She pointed at the three doors.

"I'll just show you . . ."

He slid a key into his lock. Her small sneakers were just inches from him, shining white, with a rose on each side. The flowers bloomed on wavy green stems, and there was something magical about the way the stems curved, as if they undulated in an alternate reality without right angles. He opened the door to his room. They stepped inside. He flicked the light switch to reveal four blank walls, a neat bed with one pillow, a desk with a bare surface, a chair, and a bureau. It struck Sophie as Steve Jobs–like, radical minimalism.

"Can I have a tour?" she asked.

The absurdity of it amused him. What was there to tour? Jake walked toward the standard-issue desk, light wood grain. He pulled out the chair.

"Well, *here*, you have my desk."

"You ever study here?"

Was it hot in here? Was Sophie comfortable?

"No, ma'am."

Ma'am? Was he that nervous? He knocked on the hard wooden seat. He glanced at the slice of common room beyond his door, highlighting everything his room wasn't—carpeted, visited, rich with things. He'd never had a girl in here before. Sophie looked beautiful. It had always been so easy to talk to her—to leak his mind into the air between them—but now he was consumed with inhibiting himself. He'd never had sex, not even close, but now that he was an arm's length from her, one shut door away from complete privacy, it was all he could imagine. A slideshow played in his mind, each frame a different possibility.

"Is it loud out in the hall?" Sophie asked.

It was silent.

"Maybe I should shut the door," she said as she pulled it closed. "There we go. Sorry, I couldn't hear you. So loud."

He laughed, relieved she'd only been kidding to bring them closer and hadn't somehow heard his thoughts. And as if she'd just leaned perilously toward him, as if she needed him to restore her balance, he walked toward her and kissed her. Sophie blinked out his two windows of starry sky. With their lips locked, their minds fixated on the short seam connecting them, he reached for her waist. Under her shirt, her skin felt warm, buttery. He pressed his hips into her. She was kissing him as much as he was kissing her, a Möbius strip of an embrace.

Sophie wiped her mouth, eyes rapt.

"Is that what you've been studying in Bass?" she asked.

He laughed.

She kissed his cheek.

"I interrupted you," she said.

"Hm?"

"The *tour*."

"Oh. Right."

"May I?" She gestured to his bed.

He nodded eagerly. She sat.

"What else is there to know here?" she asked.

Her smile was infectious.

"Well." He sat next to her, obedient. "I guess there's the thinking behind all of it. It's not a lot of *stuff*, but I don't want to decorate until I'm where I'm supposed to be." He'd never said that out loud. "Does that make sense?"

Sophie shook her head no.

"You mean . . . ?" she probed.

"I don't know. When there's enough."

"And when will that be?"

"I don't know. I figure I'll know when I'm there."

Sophie yawned—and covered her mouth fast, embarrassed by the reflex.

"It's just my heart, don't worry about it," he teased.

She laughed. "Sorry. I usually just go to bed after we study."

"Same," he admitted. "Do you want to stay here?"

She bit her lip. "Here here?"

He laughed. "You don't—"

"Yes," she said.

Jake walked to the bureau and removed his most expensive gym shirt—PUMA, the animal leaping over the A—and smallest joggers. Their hands brushed as he gave them to her. She changed in the bathroom while he slipped into gray sweats. They reunited to brush their teeth. She used the pair to his brush, which he found still in its plastic package.

While she used the bathroom a final time, Jake folded her shirt and jeans in a pile on his desk as carefully as he made his bed. He sat on his quilt, calm, happy. When she returned, she turned off the light, but they stayed lit dark blue by starlight as they slid into bed. His body curled into an S shape behind hers. He listened for her to say something. She only squeezed his arm. He kissed the back of her head and felt his first urge to say *I love you*, holding his tongue and savoring her until the moment they fell asleep.

Jake's phone alarm rang at 6 a.m., shattering the early morning with its repetitive hacking. He reached past Sophie, pressed *stop*, and resumed his position of a second before. Sophie lay in his arms: soft, small-boned. He kissed the nape of her neck where her hair was thin and private under all the wild yellow waves. He wondered if she were still on the hazy edge of her own dreams, feeling his kiss across consciousnesses, until she turned around. Faint freckles spread across her nose like beige Milky Way dust. Natural blush pinked her cheeks. He slid his hands up her shirt, where he could feel her ribs. Sophie gazed at him, so at ease that he knew she would let him do anything.

"You're distracted," Professor Malchik announced.

Sophie's mind had been in Jake's room, remembering the coziest she'd ever been, skin-to-skin with the softest furnace, her back arched under the thinnest sheets. Now, she returned to Professor Malchik's office. He sat at the round table, legs crossed in bland khakis. The line of buttons up his white oxford was stiff as a spine up the front of his body.

Sophie pretzeled her legs in stretchy jeans. Her two French braids looked neat in front, but had the appearance of self-tying in the back, twisting up her scalp. Her problem set lay between them filled with her notes. Some of her letters curled like vines at the ends—floral, feminine writing with an aura of far, far away. They'd been going through her work as usual, but Sophie's eyes had been wandering all afternoon.

He checked his watch: only half an hour into their two, but almost through the whole problem set. He'd kept turning the pages, hoping one would ignite her. Was she bored? Why? Today's lesson was exceptional. He'd asked Sophie to read about how people perceived time passing faster or slower depending on their emotions. They'd discussed time in states of: awe, flow, boredom, desire, grief, and, most recently, surprise.

When people were stunned, the brain's amygdala worked overtime to record more memories than usual from the unfolding scene. This more detailed reel of life made people feel as if time slowed down. He'd listed a dozen articles on the subject—all in 8-point type, because smaller fonts made people concentrate more, and he wanted Sophie to engage with this as much as possible.

Professor Malchik flipped the page to the last one—dead blank. Below the title "Fear and Time Perception," he'd listed six articles to read and left inches of white space for her thoughts. The page was still white.

"Did you see this question?" he asked.

She nodded.

"Do you want to come over?" Sophie remembered his voice. She'd looked down at this page and thought she'd finish it later. She remembered the tour. *"It's just my heart, don't worry about it."* She grinned at the memory—

"Is this funny to you?" Professor Malchik asked.

"No, sir."

She hadn't called him that before and touched her throat, sensing Jake. The silence dragged on, empty as the page.

"Did you have any other thoughts?" he asked. He prepared to end early.

"What about love?"

"Excuse me?"

"It's not in the emotions you listed." She flipped back through the pages. "How does love alter the way people feel time?"

He leaned forward. "Well, love's a bit like desire." He turned back to that page, blue with her scribbles.

"No, not desire. Real love. How does that affect the way we perceive time?"

"Real love?"

She nodded.

"You're right, maybe that's closer to awe."

He turned to *that* page. Like surprise and desire, awe slowed people's sense of time. In one study listed there, people who were shown pictures of epic mountains or other panoramic landscapes—snow-covered conifers, see-through blue waters off the coast of Thailand, glaciers sparkling at sunrise—remembered more details from those images than people shown banal photographs. They also estimated more time had passed per viewing than those looking at everyday things. They perceived more time in the same duration.

Sophie shook her head.

"No, awe happens when you encounter something so big, beautiful, or complex." She pictured the Maroon Bells. "You're tempted to worship it. But real love's . . ." *between equals*. It was when you recognized someone you'd never met, because somehow you knew they were the same. Awe was submission, and love was connection. And there was more to it than that, but Sophie didn't know quite how to dignify its depth and power. She didn't want to blunder in front of Professor Malchik, so she only said, "It's different."

"All right. I suppose love's unique."

She nodded.

"I was thinking, as I was reading," she said. "Do these emotions affect our perception of time or time itself? What if being awestruck doesn't just *feel* slow, but what if the world for you actually does slow down?"

The radical thought reminded Professor Malchik of Einstein's time dilation. Einstein was the first to posit that time doesn't pass at the same rate everywhere in the universe. The force of gravity affects time in a phenomenon known as *gravitational time dilation*: the farther a clock is from a source of gravity, the faster it ticks. The closer a clock is to a source of gravity, the slower it ticks. Speed can also affect time in *velocity time dilation*: the faster an object travels, the slower its internal clock ticks. An astronaut orbiting Earth in the International Space Station for one year—at seventeen thousand miles per hour relative to the planet—will age nine milliseconds slower than he would have on Earth. Both forms of time dilation have been proven.

But *emotional* time dilation?

Professor Malchik made a note.

"Our emotions' effects on time," he repeated as he wrote. It was an intriguing idea, that time might actually pass slower when we were in love.

"Yes."

"That our emotions don't just reflect our world, but could change our world. That might be worth thinking about."

CHAPTER 5

Leaves turned pumpkin-colored, brightening paths on campus. Fleeces covered polos, and parkas followed close behind. Jake and Sophie got used to darker mornings, warmer socks, and each other. They spent more and more time together, becoming roommates in their minds. As snow started to blunt the spires of Sterling Library, like crossing a subtle border—the same terrain, now called something new—Jake's bed became "theirs."

They fell into a routine.

Their habits were their bones, structuring a shared life.

Every morning, Jake woke up at six to work out. He brought his Moleskine to Berkeley's gym to keep meticulous track of his exercises: reps and weight. He cycled through upper body, lower body, core, long run, and then intervals day, sweating through his shirt each time. He kept a close eye on his heart rate displayed on his watch and spent at least two hundred minutes a week at 140 bpm or above. His resting heart rate was 51.

After his shower, Jake woke Sophie by touching her shoulder. They got dressed every morning to "The Classics," one of Jake's playlists, filled with old soul tunes: Ray Charles's "You Won't Let Me Go," Etta James's "At Last," and others like Sam Cooke's slow and steady "Bring It On Home to Me." Sometimes Jake sang along, his voice low and impassioned as he slid his arms through flannel sleeves. Sophie chose from her clothes filling the bottom half of the bureau. Jake made the bed. Sophie arranged the three pillows she'd moved in from her room: each two feet across, faux fur. She kept them in front of Jake's stiff, plain ones.

Sometimes they parted for morning classes. Otherwise, Sophie joined him in Cold War, a large and anonymous lecture where Jake would covertly massage her back. In the curve where her neck became shoulders, he'd melt any stiffness to threads.

They ate lunch side by side.

Tuesdays and Thursdays, in Psych 101, Jake and Sophie sat in the front row. They felt a sense of loyalty to the spot. Sophie knew the material already, so she usually let her mind wander with her head tilted to the side. She noticed she was changing. She could walk around campus undaunted by other people on the paths. She ate in dining halls at peak times without nerves forcing her to leave. She called her mom less often. She didn't feel alone.

Sophie did perk up for the psych lecture devoted to love. She uncapped her gel pen when the professor promised a definition. Love, according to the famous Dr. Robert Sternberg, had three components: intimacy, passion, and commitment. Only a couple with all three had love. But "Sternberg's Theory of Love" struck her as a party trick rather than a breakthrough. Didn't this theory just replace one ambiguous word with three? Besides, it rooted love in behavior, and wasn't love beyond bodies? Stronger than arms and legs, vaster, and longer lasting? What was its connection to space and time? Had anyone ever studied love as a force?

She left the lecture more curious than she'd come.

Even with love unmapped, Sophie knew she was in love with Jake. The word had crept into their vernacular starting days after they'd met. *"I love the way you . . . say that."* And *" . . . look at me."* And *". . . touch me."* Whole-person *"love you"* took just a couple of months. Jake said it first one night in their bed. He'd been holding her waist, his thumbs touching, lost in an overwhelming rhythm, when he said, "I love you so much," so unselfconsciously that Sophie didn't react. The words had come unintentionally from so deep inside of him that even acknowledging them felt intrusive. Still, she knew what they had.

In the afternoons, Jake and Sophie studied. She read poetry that understood real love, respecting its magic and connection to something more mind-blowing and perspective-shifting than "intimacy, passion, and commitment." She liked Rumi, who wrote: "Love is the bridge between you and everything"; "Love rests on no foundation . . . with no beginning or end"; and "Lovers don't finally meet somewhere. They're in each other all along." There was truth there. She didn't understand it exactly, but the poems felt closer to wisdom than physics and psychology. She wanted to figure it out: what was this thing happening between her and Jake? He joined her every time she visited Sterling for more books. He followed her up the main tower—seven stories tall, with eight mezzanines—into the stacks, where eighty miles of shelving were crammed into 6.5 miles of aisle space. He kissed her when they were alone and hidden in the labyrinth. He helped carry books back to their place.

Sophie's sessions with Professor Malchik were virtually the only time they spent apart. She listened to "The Classics" on walks up and down Science Hill, the steep street lined with science buildings and Sloane Physics Laboratory on top. Those songs had Jake in their pulsing beats. Sophie had never sought music out before—had never been to a concert, didn't prefer one genre to another—but she loved their morning playlist, where Jake was in every note.

Meanwhile, as the temperature dropped, Professor Malchik sensed distance grow between him and Sophie. She seemed preoccupied—even though she submitted all of her homework on time and answered every question he asked. It was as if her heart and soul were in another room. If he swung at her, he had the thought that his hand might pass through her image, because *this* Sophie was an illusion and the real her was somewhere else. He made small changes to the syllabus, but nothing grabbed her.

After library closing, Jake and Sophie walked home to Berkeley under constellations Sophie named. One night, she outlined

Pisces—two fish linked by a V-shaped trail of stars—and explained the myth: a monster was about to eat Aphrodite and her son when they turned into fish and jumped into a river to escape. They tied themselves together with a cord so they wouldn't lose each other in the water. Then she pointed out Omega Piscium in Pisces, the biggest white dot above, and explained it was actually a binary star system: two stars orbiting each other. They had the same center of mass, so they'd gotten locked in each other's gravity.

Sometimes they'd detour to Durfee's, the snack spot wedged between the Yale Women's Center and the post office. Its gas station amenities didn't appeal to Jake—rotating slices of pizza, deep-fried chicken tenders, puffed bags of chips, and refrigerators full of Starbucks drinks in glass bottles—but Sophie loved the sweets. He bought them armfuls at a time: Grandma's Mini Sandwich Cremes, Little Debbie Powdered Donuts in packages of six for seventy-five cents, and Fun Dip. They'd carry the snacks home and eat them in bed over a laptop movie.

Finally, they got under the covers facing each other. She'd burrow her nose into his chest and breathe his shower-gel scent. He smelled aggressively clean, hard-scrubbed. As they paid attention to each other's bodies in the dark, Jake came to expect the exact curve of her waist, which dipped at a fingerprint-specific slope between her ribs and hipbone. She learned his chest hair spread like wings. She'd touch his chest with such attention that she learned the different patches of hard and soft between the bones, quilting over his skeleton.

As they lay in bed, releasing the day, Sophie sometimes felt Jake tense. One moment, he'd be there, alive in all ten fingers on her, and the next moment, gone. His hands would stop on her hips, stiff. She'd open her eyes and see his brow knotted and body locked, as if all his energy were being sucked up through his limbs and into his mind. It was familiar. She knew what it was like to think that intently, that fast. In those moments, she'd stroke the back of his head and teach him something about the universe. It was usually just a quick fact, but that was all it took to put the world back into perspective. She taught him that the tallest mountain in the solar system was Olympus on Mars, five times as tall as Mount Everest and over 350 miles across, the width of Arizona. Slowly, Jake would relax again and fade into sleep. Sophie followed close behind.

Overall, it was a decadent, transformative amount of time together. Sophie became convinced that there was something massive and unstudied happening between them, something more powerful than the brain, even more important than time.

One December afternoon, Jake and Sophie lay on the hammock in Berkeley's quad, enjoying a lift in the weather and the last few minutes before her session with Professor Malchik. Both looked up at white trails left by jets across the blue sky—condensed water vapor, as she'd taught him. It was the same process that cooled their breaths into small mists in front of them. Both wore zip-ups under a thick fire blanket from their room.

"How's your mom?" she asked.

"All right."

He'd told her the broad strokes plus a few details he'd only admitted once. Sophie alone knew that ever since Jake had seen his dad in Tribeca, he made a special trip every few months. He collected sweatshirts or sweatpants he didn't wear often and dropped them down the Goodwill donation chute closest to George's apartment. After all, he and his dad were the same height, close in size. New York City could be paralytically cold. There was a chance his dad would wear them. Sophie alone knew that Jake contributed to his mom's Harlem rent with a monthly Venmo of a thousand dollars, always on the last day of the month.

"Is she going to pick you up?" Sophie asked.

Winter break was two weeks away.

"Nah."

The luxury of it sounded absurd—a glittering extravagance—that his mom would neglect a workday just to join him on the Metro-North home. Jake did toy with a dream of her visiting in the spring. Campus would be green, flowering. Every place would prompt a memory he could share. Then, of course, she'd meet Sophie—although he hadn't told her about Sophie yet. What he said and how were too important. After all, he was the same age she'd been when she married his dad, making the decisions that would define her.

He couldn't mention Sophie without inviting the comparison.

His mom wasn't a romantic anymore. Since leaving George, she had abandoned her appearance, leaving her nails unpainted and graying hair undone. She had become more tightfisted than ever, but Jake didn't resent her attitude. He understood that the one man his mom loved had disappeared, changing choice by choice with new vices until he was no longer the boy she'd given her heart to when she was a girl. Trust had not done her good.

"Is she seeing anyone?" Sophie asked.

"Um." He dipped a leg over the side of the hammock and revived their back-and-forth rhythm. "She's seen this guy Mike, but . . ."

"What?"

"She called them dates, but . . ." His mom had also mentioned that Mike—a coworker at Glen Oaks—had bought her flowers. It was stated without excitement, and she'd never said what kind of flowers they were. Her heart wasn't in it. "He's more of a friend. I don't think she's looking for love right now."

"Maybe love's different when people are older."

"I don't know. I think she had real love once, and then it shattered spectacularly, so she doesn't trust the soft stuff anymore." The only thing Mom seemed to care about was setting up his career. Sophie squeezed him. "What about you? Isabel coming?"

Sophie nodded.

"So I get to meet Mama You?" he asked.

"Of course."

He kissed her forehead and listened to the quiet. Something about the school—maybe the elaborate iron gates secluding them, or the fact that he spent all his time on Sophie—felt utopian. They were in a world of their own where time passed at a different rate, maybe not at all. Sophie was peace, magic, stillness. Even cramped on a hammock, he felt like they fit perfectly together, as if they were two parts of the same person. He kissed her forehead.

"You know I love you?" Jake said.

Sophie nodded.

They kissed, at rest.

"I want you to have everything," she said.

"I want you to know everything."

That reminded him. Didn't her session with Professor Malchik start soon? He checked his watch—three thirty-two, more than half an hour since it should've begun.

"Sophie!" he said abruptly.

At Professor Malchik's round table, Sophie stared at her knees. He faced her and the wall clock he'd hung himself. Its radio signal came from the cesium atomic clock, the most accurate clock in the world, and it had read four when Sophie finally showed up today.

He cared about time.

Did she?

"Imaginary time," he prompted.

His anger filled the room like a gas with unknown effects.

"It's a way to view space-time." Her voice was low. All the questions for today involved this concept, popularized by

Stephen Hawking. "What we consider 'real time' is the past, present, and future on one plane. Imaginary time is perpendicular to that plane: it's the z axis. Theoretically, it allows for multiple things to happen at once . . ." Professor Malchik kept waiting for her to impress him. He hated how lifeless her tone was, how uninspired. She was just repeating rote information. "Imaginary coordinates are real time coordinates multiplied by the imaginary number i—" He swatted her words aside. Everything she had said was accurate, but he wanted the words to matter to her. It wasn't perfect until she cared.

"What—?" she started.

"Enough."

Sophie hadn't even apologized. She'd just kept her eyes downcast as she entered, a sign that she had no excuse.

"You're distracted."

She opened her mouth.

"Don't lie."

A white rabbit smiled on the front of her zip-up. The ends of her hoodie's drawstrings were knotted each with a red heart bead. The strange, whimsical getup reminded him of Alice's question in Wonderland, "How long is forever?" and the White Rabbit's response, "Sometimes, just one second." But Sophie's eyes weren't as bright as her outfits. She'd been doing her work, and it was always correct. But, week after week, it was less bold, less speculative.

"Do I need to remind you who you are?"

She shook her head. Her long hair swished.

"Sophie—"

"Please," she said quietly.

He sat down at his desk.

"Where's your college essay?" he demanded of his computer. He hit *return*. The monitor dawned. "You quoted Einstein. 'I want to know God's thoughts.'"

"Please, stop."

"Do you remember Shannon?" He didn't wait. "I told you about him. The day we met. It took him ten years to write his best work, but he had his first breakthrough at twenty-one. He was twenty-one years old when he published the most important master's thesis of all time. On binary switches. It made digital computers possible. Twenty-one." His monitor went black. *And how old are you?* The question burned on the tip of his tongue. She might've looked like a child, but she wasn't. "I'm here to help you. I'm *trying* to help you."

Sophie's lips wobbled.

"Is this boring to you?"

She opened her mouth.

"Don't you want to be great?"

"No."

"No?"

"It was never about that."

"What was it about?"

Silence.

"Well?" he probed.

She stared at her knees again: twin denim hills. The world was silent, but her mind roared, thinking that her motive was always about getting to the core of things, what really mattered, and what really pulled the levers of their existence. *"Be great?"* The last thing she wanted to be was different. But she said nothing. She didn't want to tear up in front of him.

"And what about me?" he went on.

She didn't look up.

"What do you think this class is for me? A checklist item?"

Professor Malchik pinched and released the bridge of his nose. Was he being too harsh? Didn't she see what she could be? The *answers* to *everything.* Were the keys to the universe gold or silver? Did they glitter? Why didn't she anymore? He reminded her how extraordinary she was. No one in Yale's history had ever been granted such a personalized tutorial as a freshman. In last year's Olympiad, only *she* had solved the problem asking for the longest string of prime numbers spaced evenly apart. The answer was 25, and each of those prime numbers was eighteen digits long. The groundwork for that problem had won another mathematician, Terry Tao, a Fields Medal back in 2006. Sophie was exceptional, and he kept saying that, but his messages didn't crack her wall. Sophie appeared closer and closer to crying, as if every compliment insulted her more. He resigned himself to the distance between them.

"I think that's enough for today."

She closed her notebook.

"But next time I want Sophie. Not whoever you're pretending to be."

*   *   *

Sophie cried soon after in Jake's arms on their bed.

"Soph," he cooed. He pulled her hands off her face to reveal leaky blue eyes speckled pink. Her cheeks were as red as the hearts on her hoodie.

"I'm a person. I'm just a person."

"What?"

He wiped her tears.

"What happened?" he asked.

"Malchik . . ."

They'd seen him together once in Commons. He was eating alone in the antisocial half of dining hall. As far as Jake knew, Sophie and her professor had been getting along. They hadn't had any breakthroughs yet, but Sophie wasn't worried. Those took time, didn't they?

Sophie gazed at Jake's quilt. Last night, right here, they'd watched *Lord of the Rings: The Two Towers* while Sophie strung peach gummies on her fingers like rings. She ate so many that the sour taste lingered to mix with her toothpaste, creating a flavor she named WarHead Mint. Jake insisted that he try it by kissing her. She dissolved into laughter as his tongue swished over hers, popping bubbles and collapsing foam.

She wiped tears with the heel of her hand.

"We can talk about it later," he said.

She nodded.

"I love you so much. You're so special."

"No."

"No?"

"I'm not special. I'm a person." She watched a displaced tear drip down her wrist. "You're the only one who doesn't make me feel different, and I don't want that to change." She looked him in the eyes. Her expression asked, *Okay?*

"Okay."

He kissed her forehead, then her nose, then her salty upper lip. He cupped the back of her neck, careful with her head, but just as careful with the rest of her. She was so clearly a person—a warm-blooded, gorgeous, touchingly tender person—and Jake was drawn to every inch. He wanted to show her that. He crawled on top of her, still kissing, so intently that neither noticed as her latest problem slipped from the bed to the ground.

CHAPTER 6

"And I met a girl," Jake told his mom freshman spring, the closest he'd come to naming Sophie. He squeezed the phone, bracing himself. He'd never mentioned a woman to his mom before. Outside his room, Berkeley's courtyard looked hopeful: white dogwoods over green grass and yellow tulips stretching in beds. Sophie was on Science Hill in a senior-level seminar.

"Mom?"

"Yes?"

He imagined her sitting with stiff posture on their living room sofa in Harlem. Maybe she'd frozen holding the Yale mug Jake had bought for her birthday.

"Can I tell you about her?"

"What?" Janice asked.

They usually talked about his grades—all A's barring an A- in logic, where Professor Rollins referred to grade inflation as

"the latest outbreak in a pandemic of participation awards."
Then he asked extensively about how she was doing. Were the
neighbors still too loud? Was the front door still left open? How
was Glen Oaks?

"Her name is Sophie."

"Okay."

"And we've been dating since school started."

"I'm sorry, who?"

"Sophie Jones. She's my year here."

"Jones," she repeated faintly.

Jake heard her typing through the phone. He imagined her
bent over her laptop on the coffee table, its shortest leg elongated by a stack of dry tea bags. He remembered the first time
he googled Sophie, the day he met her. Her shyly smiling portraits had bombarded the results. She didn't quite look at the
camera in most of the headshots.

"A Wikipedia?" Janice asked.

"Yes." He smiled.

Silence grew.

"Well?" he asked.

"She's blonde."

As quickly as it had spread, Jake's smile vanished without
leaving any trace of its warmth behind. *Blonde.* That was Janice's
recently adopted word for the women she served at Glen Oaks.
Their hair color didn't matter. Every rich woman was "blonde,"
her dismissive slur for women with easy lives.

"International Math Olympiad." Janice enunciated the

phrase from Sophie's Wikipedia as if it were an exercise in speech therapy. "Okay. I'm glad you have a friend."

"I told you. We're dating."

"Is this why you don't have a summer job lined up?"

No. She knew why. He'd spent the past six months applying for internships on Wall Street, but most of those were only open to college juniors and above. He was qualified—if only someone met him, they'd see. With Sophie's help, Jake had been plumbing Yale's alumni network and had sent hundreds of emails with his résumé attached. If he didn't get hired, he figured he'd tutor the same kinds of teenagers he used to—in $200 sneakers, wearing privilege in their boredom—and feed his bank account in the process.

"If she's in the way of your dream, she's not the one."

"I brought her up because I'd like you to meet her."

"Meet her? *You* just met her."

"I've been putting this off for a while."

"But—"

"I know. Feelings change, people change, life changes. I know, but—"

"The decisions you make now—"

"She's like me." He touched his heart. "She has the same energy. Okay? She cares about her work. She works hard. And she's the nicest, most humble, most thoughtful person I've ever met. You don't even know what she's doing with her life. She's not in the way of my dreams, she has her own, and it's important to me to talk about her with you because she's going to be around. So, I'm asking, please, could I bring her home to introduce you?"

Janice was silent.

"After you get a job."

Peter climbed Science Hill the day of his last session with Sophie, the final nail in the coffin of their disastrous year. He'd failed before, but never so slowly, so face-to-face. Every week since their December spat, she'd come in more like a ghost than before. He knew he shouldn't have raised his voice. *"Don't you want to be great?"* He'd repelled her, and the connection he'd hoped to share with her never came. Every week, she rejected him with her blankness, her guarded politeness, and her desire to do no more than asked.

He stepped into the dim physics building, to his office. *"Please, stop."* Meanwhile, his minor celebrity as her mentor in the department had faded. Other professors had noticed: Sophie had retreated to the back rows in lectures. Her work was increasingly like other top students'. She had not outshone her peers like the all-star everyone had expected her to be. Only the chair still brought her up to Peter. Today, Peter was supposed to ask Sophie if she wanted to continue her individual study next year. "She can study with anyone in the department," the chair had said. "Make sure she knows that." Peter had nodded.

His frustration had assaulted him at random: during lunch in Commons, at the podium in Time Theory, his lecture class, or on the sidewalk where Science Hill began to slope. He'd tried everything, even topics outside of time, to spark some interest. Today's problem set dealt with the Fourier transform, a technique used to map equations as sound waves—a last-minute revision. Nothing else so far had clicked. His intensity must have been repulsive. Maybe that explained why his sons had never fallen in love with school either.

Was today his last chance? At his desk, he rehearsed his proposal: *It's hard to believe this year is over . . . If you'd like to pursue an individual study as a sophomore, I speak on behalf of the department when I say we'd be more than happy to extend the tutorial. You can work with anyone, any advisor—*

A new email from Sophie:

Re: PHYS991

Dear Professor Malchik,

I attached my problem set for this week.

I am unable to make our session today, but I wanted to thank you sincerely for your valuable mentorship this year. I am extremely grateful for the privilege of studying with you. I learned more than I could have imagined.

Thank you again.

Sincerely,

Sophie

Peter stared at the email.

In his mind, the apeirogon went dark.

He felt as if he'd lost her for good.

*   *   *

The hour before, Jake and Sophie had been reading in bed when he got an email from Lionel Padington, granting Jake a summer job interview the following day at 1 p.m.

Lionel—the most famous CEO they'd emailed in Bass. He'd been one of the few Sophie recognized. Just his name conjured his Southern accent, salt-and-pepper crew cut, and charm softening his sharp suit. Always quicker-witted than the news anchor, he lit up every TV interview. They'd found Lionel's email address in the alumni directory and inquired about a job at Padington open to college graduates. It had been bold, but so was Lionel. He'd grown his firm from nothing to manage over $50 billion. He played basketball with Jeff Bezos at the Equinox on the Upper West Side. He lived in a world of "definitely."

Now, Jake's dark eyes glowed. Sophie squeezed his ribs. They shook each other, thrilled and celebrating before the implications hit.

"Tomorrow," Sophie repeated.

Jake nodded.

She didn't even consider seeing Professor Malchik. Jake's dream felt like theirs. For the next few hours, they threw themselves heart-first into frenzied, kamikaze preparation. They rehearsed Jake's answer to every standard ask until Sophie suggested they eat dinner. Later, she asked harder questions. *"How did you choose the companies in your own portfolio?"* *"Where is the world heading?"* Sophie's stamina endured even after Jake brushed his teeth limply at 2:30 a.m. She wanted nothing more than for him to get this job. She knew how much Jake had idolized Lionel in high school. His future deserved to gleam.

He spit white foam and rinsed his toothbrush.

"Where do you want to be in ten years?" she asked.

He imagined Sophie ten years older.

"I love you," he said.

"I know."

They got into bed facing each other. His hard chest squished her nose, flattening the turned-up tip of cartilage. She crept up to his mouth and kissed the acute corner of his lips, a part of him she'd never felt before.

"Did you miss your session with Malchik?" he asked suddenly.

She crept back down.

"We're meeting tomorrow," she lied.

"Okay." He kissed her forehead. "Thank you."

She rubbed the back of his head.

"You do so much for me," he went on. "How can I be a better boyfriend?"

"By going to sleep."

"I'm serious."

"I don't know. What about me?"

"Nothing. Absolutely nothing."

As their breaths slowed, Sophie gazed at his profile backlit by stars. His nose slanted like an arrowhead. His soul had the same palpable sense of direction. No one else was as good as Jake. He'd stayed loyal to goals so far away. Who else had that focus at their age? That balance of passion and order? Who else was so ambitious and so kind? She hadn't known there was anyone else like her, but she'd found him and didn't need more. She was happy just to be.

The morning felt like ten minutes.

At last in Lionel's office—the end of a road beginning in his dreams—Jake panicked. Even sitting down, Lionel was a foot taller than Jake expected. The top-floor view was dizzying. Jake had only just bought his suit off the rack at Bergdorf's, and the tags were still on, awaiting its return. Every snaggy desk corner was now a $999 threat. Standing next to a photo of Warren Buffett, Jake was so nervous that he launched into an impromptu spiel before Lionel even said hello. He detailed his portfolio over glossy color printouts, from inception through today. His pot, now $25,090, had never dipped more than 4 percent in any month. He explained that his stock-picking method was to bet on history: Apple, Walmart, Google, and other giants had left their steps to success in plain sight. Jake looked for companies on similar paths. He bought only a few and prepared to hold them for decades. The best investments required time.

"Good afternoon," Lionel greeted after Jake finished.

"Sir, right. Hello."

"That's all very impressive, except for the bit about time."
Jake furrowed his brow. "If waiting's so important, then why
didn't you? You launched right into your spiel without introducing yourself. I'm Lionel." He laughed and offered his hand.

Jake shook it.

"Yes, sir. Sorry. I'm Jake."

"Have a seat."

Jake sat.

"You know why you're here?"

"No, sir."

"I read every résumé I get directly because I like confidence."

"Well, I have that, sir."

"You sure do. You've got a lot to learn, but I was the same
way, believe it or not."

Jake smiled, hopeful.

"You know what?" Lionel rapped the table and offered Jake a
summer job on the spot: making trade recommendations to Lionel himself. Jake's *Yes, sir* didn't leave room for even a space after
Lionel's final question mark. As if through a wormhole, Jake found
himself on the street, hands quivering. He called Sophie and told
her everything: from the lobby's turnstiles to how exuberantly val-
idating it had felt to accept Lionel's offer. Her thrill doubled his.
Her presence with him on the street was invisible but powerful.

"I love you," he said.

"I know."

He called Janice next and broke the news. He couldn't remember the last time she'd sounded so joyful. Then, time

slowed. He reminded her that a job meant she would meet Sophie. He tasted sour silence after that, hard to swallow.

"Fine," Janice agreed.

"Would Friday work?"

That Friday, Jake fidgeted with Sophie's hand all the way into New York City, as they sat side by side on the Metro-North. Their windows framed blurry green suburbs: impressionistic Milford, then Darien. Sophie wore a blue wrap dress, its scalloped hem printed with waves. For once, she'd brushed a neat middle part into her long hair.

Of course Janice would love her.

So why was he fidgeting?

He reached for his earbuds, handed one to Sophie, and gave them "The Classics."

The melody of "Stand by Me" soothed him.

Sophie had heard so much about Jake's neighborhood by then that the rest of the trip verged on déjà vu: off at Harlem–125th Street station and then onto an uptown subway to 168th Street, where they surfaced between a McDonald's and a Duane Reade. They exited with their backpacks, planning to spend the night at an Airbnb before apartment hunting tomorrow. They passed an unnamed restaurant advertising $1 PIZZA SLICE, OPEN 24 HOURS next to an awning claiming GROCERY & CANDY. Heat waves rose off the bus lane.

Jake stopped suddenly.

"You okay?" Sophie asked.

He gazed at his mom's rectangle in the building's grid of dark windows. He and Janice had never had guests over before. He nodded yes and stepped forward to buzz 3C under a layer of graffiti. The door rattled. Sophie stepped inside first, grinning, unthwarted by the waft of marijuana. They creaked upstairs until Janice came into view in the doorway, her arms crossed over a denim button-up. She looked only at Jake, silently ecstatic. As they hugged—reunion energy lifting everyone's spirits—he kept holding Sophie's hand. He leaned back first.

"Mom, this is Sophie."

"So great to meet you!" Sophie radiated sincerity.

Janice smiled hard.

"Come in," she managed.

Jake and Sophie held hands as they entered. Without turning around, he led Sophie on a guided tour: every photo in the living room including the framed sketch of Janice he'd drawn as a toddler. Sophie was rapt. Jake did call over to Janice a couple of times, but not with anything substantive. *"Right, Mom?"* And, *"That fair?"* The way he and Sophie clung to each other, Janice had never seen him so . . . dependent. He tucked a strand of hair behind Sophie's ear. She rubbed Jake's bicep. They never stopped touching. Janice just stood there and answered Jake's questions with monosyllables. She opened and shut the oven—she had to do *something* more than loiter— fanning fragrant steam into the air. The smell of chicken lured

Jake into the kitchen. He kissed Sophie's forehead beside a table set for three.

"Your hair's off," Janice said.

"What?" Jake looked at Sophie, who squirmed with non-opinion. He found his reflection in the microwave and realized he'd been running his hand so nervously over his scalp on the train that he'd tousled his hair into waves. Janice patted his hair back into crisp alignment.

"There," Janice said. "Messy hair, messy life."

"Gotta fix that before my first day."

They slid into easy conversation about Lionel. Janice asked every question. When would Jake start? Next week. How much would they pay? Ten thousand dollars for two months of work. During that pause, she ushered Jake and Sophie to sit down. She served everyone a plate of chicken, roasted broccoli, and Uncle Ben's rice pilaf from the microwave.

"Was he nice?" Sophie asked.

"Definitely. I mean, he actually wants to *help*." Jake forked chicken into his mouth. "He wants to develop me. Get to know me. Make me his protégé or something. It's crazy. Have you ever heard of something like that?"

"Only once," Sophie admitted.

She pictured Professor Malchik.

"Well, it'll be good to have you back here," Janice said.

She nodded her head at his room.

Jake tensed.

"Sophie and I were planning to live together."

"Oh?"

"She'll be working here, too."

"And what will you do?" Janice's tone was hard-edged.

"I'll be at Free People."

Janice crossed her arms.

"The store? Jake said you study physics?"

"She does," Jake intervened.

"I'm talking to her," Janice said. "And what will you do at Free People?"

"Inventory."

"What does that have to do with physics?" Janice asked.

"Mom," Jake said.

"I'm just curious why she chose it."

"I was waiting to see where Jake got hired first."

"Ah," Janice said.

"She'll study physics on her own," Jake butted in. "The job'll be easy enough that she'll have the downtime to think and read what she wants to during the day. Plus, it'll keep her weekends free." Janice scowled. "What? What's that look?"

"So she took the job not to do it."

"No, that's not it."

Sophie looked at her hands as they argued. Jake wasn't wrong, but he wasn't quite right either. The truth was that she cared less and less about the questions that used to keep her up at night: What really controls us? What plucks the strings of the universe? What is the real power of love? The best she could describe it—and she hadn't yet—was that her energy had shifted down from her head and into her heart. She was on another wavelength: genuinely content. By the end of the year, her mind was wandering in even her smallest seminars, imagining what movie she'd watch with Jake next. She'd chosen Free People without angst because work was finally just a job. She only wanted one with good enough pay, close to home, because her greatest joys were no longer her greatest insights. Her bliss came from time with Jake.

"What do you want to do after graduating?" Janice interrogated.

Sophie looked at Jake.

"She wants to figure out how the world works," Jake said so aggressively that it stifled all noise. He stood to rinse his plate in the sink. Sophie excused herself to the bathroom, left the room with her head bowed. The door shut.

"Well?" Jake whispered.

"Well what?"

"What's the matter?"

Silence.

He leaned toward Janice.

"Mom?" he said.

"She's not what I expected."

"Excuse me?" he asked.

His eyebrows flew up.

"You said she had her own dreams."

"Of course she does."

"You can't see people the way they really are when you're in love with them. Remember, the decisions you make now—"

"I know exactly who she is."

Janice's mouth was a firm line. "She's just pretty, and you're not thinking straight. Come on, Jake. She wants to 'figure out how the world works?'" Janice shook her head. "She's not going to figure that out any sooner than I am."

The toilet flushed.

Sophie returned.

Jake stood, still riled.

"Thanks for dinner, Mom. Tonight was special for me."

"Jake—" Janice started.

"I'm sorry we have to head out."

Their subway car downtown was empty except for a man sleeping across a row of seats. The soles of his sneakers had split from the toes. Jake glanced at the face. *Not him.*

"Was I okay?" Sophie asked.

"Of course."

He kissed her forehead.

"She loves you very much," Sophie said.

"I know."

So why hadn't Janice loved Sophie?

One of his fears had been that Sophie would be paid too much attention. But *"just pretty"*? Jake had never expected that. Maybe the problem was that no one was impressive up close. From one second to the next, everyone was a boring human being. You couldn't tell if someone was a genius just from watching them eat chicken, broccoli, and rice. People distinguished themselves over years, not over a single meal.

Still, something wasn't right.

Jake realized that even though he wanted people to *treat* Sophie normally, he wanted them to know she wasn't. Because Sophie was beyond special. She was a generational event. The depth of her mind was matched only by the depth of her heart.

CHAPTER 7

Jake and Sophie rose, fingers braided, in the elevator up to Lionel's penthouse. Sophie stood on strappy high heels, the first she'd ever worn. They'd been a twentieth-birthday gift from Isabel, arriving with a note that said, *Be irresponsible!* in swirling script. Sophie's black A-line dress was short but modest. She looked like she might've been on her way to class—except for the shoes. Jake pumped her hand.

"I've missed you," he said.

"I know."

It was a month into junior fall, and they'd barely talked since school started—even though they lived together. Jake was working part-time for Lionel. They'd converted one of the two bedrooms in their double into a shared office that replaced Bass in their routine. Jake's work for Lionel came in waves, and the last had just ebbed. During that weeklong frenzy, Jake had slept less than four hours a night, only finishing the company analysis that morning at the tail end of an all-nighter. He'd napped for most of their train ride into the city.

The elevator opened to Lionel's fiftieth birthday party where the fancy mob shocked Sophie. One hundred overlapping conversations rang like an alarm, loud and frightening. Shiny suits and glittery dresses lit up the enormous living room. She and Jake had never been to a party this big. She doubled her hold on him, grabbing his arm with her unheld hand.

"You okay?" he asked.

She nodded.

He kissed her forehead.

"There they are."

Jake nodded toward Lionel and his wife, Giulia, a few paces away. Lionel looked like an older version of Jake: fit and confident. He was in the middle of a story captivating a few guests. Giulia, an Italian beauty, smiled elegantly in a floor-length gown. Lionel spotted Jake and, if possible, perked up. Sophie felt Jake's posture lift—the way a child might stand taller onstage when his parents joined the audience. Lionel returned to his story.

On the way to the deck, Sophie took in several women's faces, both old and unwrinkled. Plastic surgery, most likely. Sophie wondered why they didn't let their bodies change. The idea that some people felt valued only for their faces seemed terribly sad. What about their interests and dreams? Their internal intricacies? How deeply they loved? She felt lucky to be with Jake as they walked through open French doors. Under hanging lanterns, they leaned on railing overlooking the city. Jake took her hand, kissed her knuckles three times.

"Would you decorate this place?" she asked.

He smiled. She'd remembered his rule not to decorate until he landed for good.

"We'll see," he said.

He kissed her cheek.

"So what does Lionel know about me?" she asked.

He searched his memory with visible effort. The first thing he'd ever told Lionel about Sophie was that she studied time. Jake remembered that moment in detail because Lionel had been so confused. "It's a topic in physics," Jake had explained proudly in Lionel's office. During the summer, they'd met there every day at Lionel's request after the markets closed. "She thinks time is the least understood, most important thing in the world." Sophie had never said that exactly, but that was how Jake had interpreted her interest. Since then, he and Lionel had talked so much, he must've said thousands of things about her.

"Smart. He knows you're smart. I talked about you at the beginning." Then it had become work talk.

"Jake, my boy!"

Lionel's deep voice made them turn.

"Sir!"

The two men shook hands like swinging baseball bats, clapping midway between them.

"Thanks for making the trip," Giulia said.

"The kid hasn't left!" Lionel said. "My in-box, that is."

Jake looked at Sophie.

"Sir, Giulia, this is my girlfriend, Sophie Jones."

Lionel had been looking forward to this. Jake had been singing Sophie's praises for years. Her Wikipedia page read like science fiction. But even more fascinating, something happened to Jake every time he mentioned her. Normally, Jake was specific. Whenever he mentioned a stock price, he named it to two decimal points. But when Jake talked about Sophie, he was vague. *"Special." "Incredible."*

"Lionel Padington." He extended a hand. Sophie shook it quickly, then pulled her arm back and held it bent on her chest as if in a sling.

"Giulia Padington."

Sophie nodded.

" 'The Next Einstein!' " Lionel cued.

Sophie's smile wobbled.

Lionel cleared his throat.

"Jake said you study time?" Lionel asked.

Jake sensed her discomfort. Was it Lionel's importance to him? Their work relationship aside, she knew the care he'd taken in getting to know Jake. Jake had told him unvarnished stories about Harlem and Tribeca. They flagged news articles to each other every morning and forwarded each other headlines about Yale's sports wins suffixed with their own commentary. They'd competed in the Mighty Montauk Triathlon together in July. Lionel was a key person in Jake's life whom Sophie checked on in daily conversation: *"How's Janice?" "How's Lionel?"*

Now, she gazed inward.

"I did," Sophie said at last.

Lionel leaned forward an inch.

"Oh?" He put a hand in his pocket.

Sophie didn't offer more.

"So, what's next?" he asked.

Her cheeks turned pink.

"Well," Lionel said, his tone gentler. "I must've lost my manners and skipped right over the basics. Please excuse me. Where are you from?"

She opened her mouth.

"New York."

"City?" Lionel asked.

"No, Westchester."

"How are you liking New Haven?"

"It . . ." Sophie started.

A beat.

It became clear she wasn't going to speak.

"Well, we won't hog you for the whole evening." He patted Jake affectionately on the shoulder. "Sophie, you're an impressive one. I look forward to hearing what you get into next. The next 'least understood, most important thing in the world.'" He winked at Jake.

"Love," Sophie said.

"Hm?" Lionel asked.

"The least understood, most important thing in the world is love."

Giulia raised an eyebrow. She'd been as eager as Lionel to talk to Sophie. A neurosurgeon, she loved meeting ambitious young women in the sciences and was eager to help them achieve their goals. For someone with Sophie's credentials, she'd expected a sharp, analytical mind. Wasn't this girl on the edge of knowledge? Looking over the line between the known and unknown? She'd expected to learn something from Sophie—about time, the universe, or mankind. For Sophie to say something maudlin was disappointing.

"What did she say?" Lionel asked Giulia.

"Love," Giulia said.

"Love. Right."

Sophie's pink cheeks turned red.

"Well, coming from you, it's very *Good Will Hunting*," Giulia said. She was still smiling politely when slick-haired Tony joined the group. Sophie recognized him from Jake's descriptions: the Harvard grad who wore too much hair gel and got sloppy drunk at work parties. Tony did decent work and was a scratch golfer, but there was a fratty side to him that didn't click with Jake. Tony stirred a drink.

"*Good Will Hunting*?" Tony probed.

"Tony!" Lionel greeted.

"What's all this about *Good Will Hunting*?"

"Sophie, Jake's girlfriend, was a math prodigy," Giulia explained. "Now, she thinks love is the most important force in the world."

"Ah. Now you're 'gonna see about a girl?'"

"Tony," Lionel sniped. "For Christ's sake."

"What? Matt Damon doesn't take the job. He says, 'I'm gonna see about a girl.'" No one concurred. "Am I on mute? The deadbeat genius."

"All right, calm down." Lionel didn't want to watch Tony bludgeon Sophie's sensitivity with a hammer. "Great to meet you, Sophie. Boys."

Sophie's legs hung between Jake's as he stared out the train window. Yellow towns scrolled by in silence. They'd left the penthouse soon after chatting with Lionel. It had been a sprint to make the 9:01 p.m. Metro-North back to New Haven. She and Jake had barely spoken on the crowded subway to Grand Central. Now, sitting down, her ankles ached in red Xs under her shoe straps. She touched one of the wounds. The night had left its mark. She'd been unable to speak a full sentence to Jake's godsend, the man who'd gifted him with a job, so much of his time, and enormous, priceless faith. But Jake knew that side of her already, right? He knew everything about her. So why was he acting so stunned?

"Jake?" she whispered.

His distance was odd. The night train rumbled like a washing machine.

"The least understood, most important thing in the world is love?" Jake shook his head. He'd never heard Sophie say anything like that. The words stuck with him like flakes in a snow globe, drifting and unable to settle.

"Jake?" she asked again.

She poked him.

He flinched with surprise.

"What?" he asked.

"What is it?"

His eyelashes looked soft up close. From root to tip, they were the same length as his meticulous haircut. She wanted to kiss his eyelid, but the mood was strange. He turned back to the window and stared at ghost towns.

"Introducing you to other people . . ." He kept his hands on her knee. His profile was distinct. "I saw you as they do, you know?"

"What do you mean?"

"I don't know."

"Yes, you do."

"You've changed since we met."

He hadn't pieced it together until the judgment left his lips: she didn't study with Professor Malchik anymore. She didn't take any advanced classes. She only enrolled in large, "Introduction to . . ." lectures, and she didn't seem to care about any of them. She never read physics for fun anymore. She used to want to figure out the universe. "The least understood, most important thing in the world is love?" When had her dream disappeared?

"Everyone's changing," she said. "We're growing up."

"Yeah."

He couldn't let it go.

"But that thing you said about love?"

"Nikola Tesla said, 'If your hate could be turned into electricity, it would light up the whole world.'" She'd read that freshman year. "But what about love? What is love capable of? Some of the best thinkers have started work on love as energy, or on love as a force, but no one's broken through. At the same time, there's so much out there about how love changes people." She'd read about the addictions people beat for a loved one; the miles traveled, years spent waiting, and the physical and mental transformations endured. Behind every great feat, there seemed to be a great love. Something about it could propel people up to higher levels of life. "It's an area begging to be known. I used to think I'd be the one to do it."

Sophie remembered that phase. Freshman year, when she and Jake fell in love—and she finally felt accepted, an unimaginable peace—she started to believe that love was the most powerful, most important thing in the universe. In an effort to understand it, she read poetry that echoed what she was feeling. After a while, though, true connection was so fulfilling, she lost the desire to grasp its power. She was content with a simple life.

Meanwhile, Jake latched on to the phrase *"used to."* He squeezed her hand, feeling sad. Had he done this? She had the same passion, the same intellect; they just weren't fueling a goal. He'd always loved her mind, but her lack of ego was keeping her from using it.

"Are you happy?" he asked.

"Of course!"

She smiled.

"If she's in the way of your dream, she's not the one." But what if he was in the way of hers? For the first time, Jake breathed life into the thought of who they would be apart. The idea cut him deep. Sophie gave him complete intimacy, complete companionship, and complete freedom while he threw himself into his goals. She wasn't chasing her own vision the same way anymore, but she understood what it was like to need to. She understood wanting to do something important, something specific, and to invest everything in that dream because she was the exact same way. They just understood. And their *connection.* They were ingrained in each other's habits. She was almost always with him and always in his heart. Could he ever tolerate being alone again? After knowing what it was like to fuse with someone else?

In all of Jake's ideas for the future, their family was core to his vision. They hadn't made any plans, only dreams. A couple of times, they'd been lying in bed and her hair happened to fall across his chest, painting a sunny sash across his torso. He'd picked up a strand and laid it above his lips in the image of their son. Jake suggested the name Fabio. She insisted on Legolas. Both made her laugh, hard as the rib-tickling she pretended to hate. He loved that sound and wanted to hear it every day for the rest of his life. Neither one of them had questioned that they'd always be together. They'd talked about living in New York when they were older, close to their parents. The more he worked now, the more they could share in the future. He really did believe this was just a phase. One day, they would decorate—but what would Sophie do until then? What could he give her in the meantime and what was he taking away?

"What is it?" she asked.

"I love you so much."

"I know." She looked puzzled.

"I'm probably just tired."

The conductor punched their tickets, moved to the next row.

"I just need to relax," Jake said.

She kissed his thumb.

"Can you teach me something?" he asked.

She brightened—they only had this conversation in their closest moments. Jake leaned on her shoulder while her mind flipped through shots of outer space. She pictured the planet thirty-three million light-years away covered in burning ice; then, Hubble Telescope views of green and magenta clouds a hundred million light-years away, where matter was so dense that each tablespoon weighed one billion tons; and then, the hundreds of millions of planets with conditions to support life. As Sophie traced the veins on Jake's hand, pictures of the enormous, the magnificent, and the strange faded. On their little blue dot in space, at an insignificant moment in their short lives, she couldn't think of anything greater than the feeling of just being with him. Her fingertips on his warm skin was her entire world, and her mind was consumed with touch.

"Okay, something about touch?" she suggested. He nodded. "Americans touch each other a lot less than people do in other cultures. In France and Latin America, for example, people touch each other hundreds of times an hour in public."

"I feel like I'm always touching you."

Their four hands became a focal point.

"We're an exception," she said, sensing Jake calm down more with every word. "In America, couples touch each other less than ten times an hour. At the same time, twenty percent of those in relationships don't feel loved. I think touch is part of the solution. When two people touch each other, their nervous systems relax: stress, heart rate, and blood pressure all come down. We feel less fear, less pain. There's actually a correlation between time spent cuddling and how well your immune system is functioning." She stroked his hand. "But what I find *most* interesting about touch is the shared part of it. You can't touch without being touched. You can't be touched without touching, and the benefits are the same in both directions. So, if I'm touching you, or if you're touching me, it has the same effects on each of us. It's like Newton's third law: For every action, there's an equal and opposite reaction."

"Is Fabio gonna be as smart as you?"

"What do you mean?"

"Or is he gonna be a dumb animal like me?"

"You're no dumb animal." She stroked his arm and was passively stroked in return. Finally, she felt him relax, but his peace was too new and delicate—now was not the time to mention she'd run into Professor Malchik that afternoon.

* * *

Hours earlier, Peter had been looking at his square of lasagna, but saw Sophie. The scalloped edge of his pasta was a screen for his projected memory. He'd spotted her leaving a physics class that afternoon and stopped short in the hallway. Her email freshman spring—I am unable to make our session—was still their most recent exchange. The few steps between them felt enormous. A black Nike tee dwarfed her tiny jean shorts. It didn't look like anything she used to wear. She waved but said nothing. The shirt billowed as she left.

How did they get into this stalemate? He used to imagine sitting in the front row of her Fields Medal award ceremony. Now, he only heard about her through the grapevine. Apparently, she'd shown up so late to a midterm exam in electricity and magnetism, she hadn't finished. Sometimes, in the middle of his seminar, Professor Kotak found her zoned out with a dopey smile. Had she gotten into drugs? Opiates? It was a startling loss of ambition, as if she'd found the answers to all her burning questions and was content to live unstimulated. Meanwhile, Peter had returned to the life he had before he met her, left to wonder where her heart had gone.

After this afternoon, however, Peter was sure she was seeing someone. That shirt was clearly not her own. He kept coming back to that point. Her style was so much younger, brighter than that black box hiding her like a candle snuffer.

Benji cut into his lasagna.

Zack chewed green salad.

Peter hardly noticed his family around the dinner table. Instead, he wondered how long Sophie had been dating the man implied by her outfit. Had she been on her way to meet him earlier? Had he asked her to skip class? Was he a prodigy, too?

"No Rachel tonight?" Maggie asked.

Benji shook his head.

"We broke up," he said.

Zack stopped chewing.

Maggie put her fork down.

Rachel, Benji's girlfriend for the past year, had come over almost every day after school. Even Peter had liked her. She had endeared herself to him by slapping Benji whenever he said something unusually stupid in the house. *Is melted cheese a food or a drink?* Slap. *Seriously. I don't chew it at all. What is it?* Slap.

Peter was stunned and, with Sophie still at the forefront of his mind, he worried about the relationship he'd only just started to see. He imagined the owner of that Nike shirt leaving her as callously as Benji had left his girlfriend. It angered him.

Only Benji kept eating.

"Dude," Zack said.

"What?"

"What happened?" Zack asked.

Benji dragged a stiff finger across his neck.

"Benji," Maggie chided.

"Answer the damn question!" Peter snapped.

Everyone swiveled to face him at the head of the table. No one knew he'd been listening to—let alone was invested in—their conversation. His lasagna remained untouched. Now, he stared at Benji. His mind had returned from its trek to animate his eyes.

"What happened?" Peter repeated.

"Dude, what do you want me to say?" Benji demanded. "Like, you want me to say what happened between me and her?"

"Yes."

"Look, I don't even know. One minute, we're dating. The next, it feels different." He shrugged. "Can I go back to my dinner now?"

"Is she okay?" Peter asked.

Benji blinked. His dad rarely paid him any attention. When he did, it was usually with drudgery tapering into a yes-or-no question.

"I have no idea," Benji said.

"That's cold, bro," Zack said.

"Everyone handles it differently," Maggie said gently.

"Look, I dated her for a year already. Actually more than that, because she got me an anniversary gift. My point is I'd like a day off please." He squeezed an empty bottle of ketchup onto his plate, squelching out a long fart noise without expelling any condiment. He squeezed again. "Ma, this ketchup is *fucked*."

Peter pushed his plate forward.

*　　　*　　　*

That night, Maggie and Peter did the dishes side by side at the sink. While Maggie loaded the dishwasher, rinsed plate by rinsed plate, Peter scrubbed the lasagna pan. He was rubbing the brush in circles when Sophie's new shirt superimposed itself over the foam.

"I know you're upset about Benji and Rachel," Maggie said as she closed the dishwasher. It rained behind the door at her hip. "I am too. But they weren't right for each other. They'll both find someone better suited. It happens."

Peter scrubbed harder.

"She'll be okay," Maggie said.

"You don't know that," Peter said, on another wavelength entirely. He wasn't sure Sophie would be all right. Men her age—in the same bracket as Benji—could be selfish, careless, dense. He didn't want her to suffer their faults. She'd always been so attuned to details. It hurt him to think how reactive she might be to something as massive as heartbreak. Only one question stuck with him as he rinsed the pan of soap: had she chosen someone kind?

CHAPTER 8

Sophie stood next to Jake in their office about to interrupt him. The view might as well have been through a telescope for how distant he seemed.

Jake slouched in his sleek new chair, typing. He used to sit in the Yale-issued wooden one, but that hard seat wasn't made for as much use as Jake gave it. So, a few months ago that fall, after three summers at Padington, Jake had bought a $79 replacement. Its spine curved between two cushions propping him up for his latest challenge. Jake had been managing $200,000 of Lionel's personal money since senior year began, the most he'd ever handled at once. If he returned more than the S&P 500 by graduation, Lionel would seed him with $1 million to start his own investment fund. So, Jake had been working in that chair more than he slept in their bed. Now, one foot in front of Sophie, he was light-years away in one of his states: dead still except for his impassioned fingers. His whole life was in his hands.

"Jake?" Sophie asked.

Nothing.

"Jake. *Jake.*"

He turned his chin but not his eyes.

"Hey. Sorry."

That day, Jake had only left his new chair for water from the bathroom and napkin-wrapped food from the dining hall. He'd been working fanatically on Yetsa, a software company and major investment whose stock price had dropped 20 percent in a month. Jake's December 1 birthday had come and gone since Yetsa started its decline. He'd been postponing their celebration for two weeks. On the few occasions he'd left this room to go outside, he'd felt like he was intruding from a different reality. Everyone was so slow, too calm—even Sophie. Tonight, though, he'd promised her time. He pushed himself away from the desk.

"All right. I'm here."

Jake kissed her cheek.

"You smell good," she said.

He stepped into the common area where they usually kept a brown coffee table from Isabel, a futon stuffed with sour candy dust, and a mini fridge. Now, the room contained only a dinner table set for two. The chairs were seated side by side. Jake held Sophie's hand and, in the dim light, pulled her close with an expression mixing love with sadness.

"This is too thoughtful," he said, stern.

She wasn't sure it was a compliment.

They sat. Sophie had forgotten what it was like to see Jake's body up close. Thick biceps stuffed his zip-up. Each of his quads spanned twice the width of hers. She remembered they hadn't kissed, not really, in a while. Sophie placed her hand on his thigh. She missed this body—*his* body, smelling artificially clean, Nike-wrapped, hard all over, with his unique pattern of chest hair. Even more, she missed the way *he* animated his body: the essence that emerged when he moved, the way he loved a good meal more than anyone else, the way he worked himself so recklessly and yet kept structure, the old soul of his music playing in the back rooms of his mind, and the way he held her waist in his two sturdy hands.

"Sorry I've been so MIA," he said. "Yetsa . . ." Jake picked up his stream of consciousness where it had stopped at his computer. While they ate—prosciutto-wrapped cod, arugula salad with pears, with two chocolate croissants for dessert waiting under a white napkin—he walked her through the debacle. In a new nervous tic, he covered his eyes sometimes with his hand as he spoke. He mentioned he'd hired an analyst in India parttime.

"I didn't know that," Sophie said.

"Really? I thought I told you."

She shook her head.

Jake stared at his empty plate.

"What about you?" he asked. "What's new?"

"I accepted a job for next year."

Jake swiveled to face her head on.

"Free People," she confirmed.

"Ah."

The sentence made him feel ill.

He pushed his plate forward.

"You need to go to grad school," he snapped.

"What?" she asked. In her vision of the future, Jake would get seeded when they graduated. They would move to Manhattan. Grad school did not fit in that picture. The best ones for physics weren't even in New York, and she just wanted to be close to him. Her job was a means to an end, not a matter of heart and soul.

"I'm going to be working all the time," Jake said.

"Where's this coming from?"

He gestured at the food. "Come on," he said.

"Jake."

"How long did this take you to make?"

Jake had never worked so hard, making the changes in Sophie more apparent than ever. She'd lost all desire for more. It wasn't right. She deserved so much more than she had—things she could only give herself. He'd been ignoring his doubts about her path for a while. Now, at his limit, he didn't have the strength to hold them back.

"You have a gift you're not using," he said.

"Don't tell me what's important to me."

Jake slid his plate off the table into the wall, where it shattered. Neither one of them moved, the room noiseless as a vacuum.

"Sophie, wake up," he snapped.

"What?"

"What happened to you?" he asked.

"I'm happy."

He considered this.

"Maybe now, but you won't be," he said definitively. "You'll regret this. Now's the time to do something with your life."

"I *am*."

Jake felt too much of himself in that sentence. He pressed his lips together, frustrated, and remembered when Sophie asked him last year, *"Do you know why lips are soft?"* She traced the squished O of his mouth in their bed. Sophie had taught him that skin had three layers. The top one—usually thick, tough—was paper-thin on the lips, making them smooth. They had more nerve endings than any other body part, making them hypersensitive. They didn't produce melanin, so there was no pigment to hide pink vessels in the dermis. All information she'd ever passed on to him was still inside her. But what good did that do if only he knew it was there?

"Sophie, I love you," he said, "but I won't let you hide from the world."

"Jake," she protested.

"This relationship is killing you."

"Babe."

"No. Something isn't right." Jake grabbed his parka from the coat rack, rattling it like a leafless tree. He slammed the door behind him. Sophie sat alone at the table for two. The ghost-white napkin in the center still covered her croissant. It cooled and hardened as Sophie went to their room, lay in bed, and called her mom.

Ringing.

Sophie and Jake always kept their blinds open. The views used to prompt her tangents on constellations in front of them, but she hadn't taught him anything in a while. Jake went to bed so much later than she did. Sophie stared at the snow-colored moon and felt cold.

"Hello?" Isabel sat up in bed.

"Mom."

"Darling, what's wrong?" Isabel left her bedroom, where Sophie's dad stayed asleep. She sensed it was about Jake.

"Jake left."

Isabel walked into the library.

"We got in a fight," Sophie went on. "He said I need to go to grad school. He thinks I'm wasting my life. He just walked out. I don't know if he's coming back."

"Of course he's coming back."

"I've never seen him so angry."

Sophie's eyes pinched out tears.

"Where are you?" Isabel asked.

"In bed."

"Deep breaths."

"What should I do?" Sophie asked.

Isabel had never given her daughter relationship advice. She had talked to Sophie about love, though, since it first appeared in her bedtime stories. *"Life is about how deeply you love and let others love you."* She must've told Sophie that dozens of times under her square of skylight. Now, Sophie wanted specifics. She wanted advice about *him.*

Isabel had first met Jake while picking Sophie up for winter break freshman year. Seeing them together—always with a point of contact between them—was like watching a heartbeat on an ultrasound. It was intense, indisputable aliveness. The force between them felt tangible, charging the air with something that pricked her lightest hairs. After Isabel met Jake, the intensity of their relationship made sense. He'd looked back into Isabel's eyes with such a spotlight glare, with such purpose, that it almost stole her breath.

It reminded her of—

"Mom?" Sophie's voice cracked.

"I had my heart broken, too." It was only when Sophie cried harder that Isabel realized she'd said that out loud. She wiped the sleep out of her eyes. "I don't mean that's what's happening now. I just meant the pain. That pain . . . It's familiar."

"What happened?"

Isabel listened to her daughter quiet down. Information had always soothed Sophie. Jake seemed to have the same trait.

"Well, I was about your age. We'd been together for a few years. Then, he left."

"Why?"

"Nothing went wrong." Isabel hadn't told this story in decades. "It took time to understand. I still don't know for sure. I think what happened was we stopped growing. We weren't developing, together or separately." Isabel thought out loud. "I think love, when you're young, is possessive. It says, 'You're mine. We must be together. You must love me back.' Or maybe that's just passion." Aidan had been a painter. He and Isabel had spent hours upon hours adding up to weeks walking through galleries together in New York City. When she passed an art museum, to this day, she sometimes dropped in as a way of being with him. After he left, Isabel tried to chase him with phone calls, letters, and urgent requests to talk *now*, did he have *just five minutes anytime in the next two weeks*. "It taught me you can't force people to love you. Either someone chooses you, or they don't. You can only control yourself."

"You don't understand."

"What is it?"

Silence.

"Sophie?"

Sophie started crying more desperately, making further conversation impossible. It was palpable hurt, as if someone had amputated her right hand. Isabel had come to believe that the smarter people were, the more deeply they felt. Sophie never withdrew because she was apathetic, it was because she felt too much. Now, as Sophie lay wounded—brilliantly so, her super-sensitized nerves reeling—Isabel wished she could feel her daughter's pain for her. She resigned herself to the fact that the most she could do to help was listen.

*   *   *

Sophie woke up when Jake came to bed. Their mattress dipped under his weight, drawing her to him. As they hugged, his heartbeat sent vibrations through her chest.

"I love you," he said.

"I know."

He touched the outer ridge of her ear, then her lobe. Sophie had never pierced her ears. She didn't have a driver's license. She didn't drink alcohol because she didn't like the taste. Once, freshman year, as they climbed Science Hill between candy-apple-red trees, she'd asked if he was going trick-or-treating without any apparent awareness that people their age didn't do that anymore. He loved her details. But on his walk around campus minutes ago, he couldn't shake the feeling that he was hurting her. He pictured her on the day they met: bright hair, magnetic mind, and for all of her potential and power, so humble in how she asked him about the ordinary parts of his life and cared about the answers. No one was as good as Sophie. He was passing Bass Library when he decided he wouldn't hold her back any longer.

"I mean it, I love you," he said.

"I know, Jake."

"Even if it doesn't look like it, I do."

Jake launched a final effort to lure Sophie back to her dream. He planted books—*A Brief History of Time*, *The Time Paradox*—in stacks hoping they'd ignite her. He subscribed to *Physics World* and left issues by her chair. When he emerged from stretches of pure focus, he hoped they'd reminded her of what she used to be like, too.

His amount of work did weigh on him, but that was when he remembered his why: he wanted *them* to have everything. He imagined their future. Maybe the jokes about Fabio had gotten to him, because he fantasized about coming home to Sophie and their son. In his mind, he'd pulled up to their driveway thirty years from now over a hundred times. The way he saw it, the sun had set. The sky was pink. Their house was the kind Sophie had grown up in, surrounded by trees. Her silhouette shaded a yellow window in the library. Their son was just out of the frame, but present. She saw Jake walking up the front steps and smiled. That dream visited him with such clarity, Jake could count the trees on their lawn. It even had a temperature: warm. His fantasies had never had a temperature before.

Looking ahead kept him going.

But Sophie did not change.

She had debilitating peace.

Slowly, reluctantly, Jake realized he would leave.

He felt soggy, weak.

Imagining the future became deeply sad.

From then on, their intimate moments were imbued with a sense of the *last time*. He could be distant when they were in their office, but when their bodies touched, without barriers or distractions, his superfocus showered her completely. Whether it happened slowly, or in fast, uncontrollable ecstasy, every one of those moments was etched with more details than weeks of normal life. He poured his heart and soul into them. He tried to memorize her.

The week before graduation, Jake was in his sleek chair on Friday night when the call finally came. Lionel's name on his cell phone jolted him upright. Sophie crept over from her chair holding a copy of *Neverwhere,* an urban fantasy by Neil Gaiman, her thumb a bookmark. Jake's Bloomberg window displayed the size of the portfolio: $238,800.13, up 19 percent since September—comfortably higher than the S&P's 13-point rise. At last, Lionel promised to seed Jake. Sophie's smile magnified the setting sun as they agreed on next steps, including Jake's plan to rent office space across the hall from Padington itself.

Jake hung up, stunned. Sophie forgot her book until it collided with the floor. She grabbed his arms and jumped up and down as he stood still.

"Jake!" she exclaimed. "Oh my God!"

She hugged him so hard that she pushed him into his chair. She fell onto his lap and kissed him up one side of his face, then on his ear an extra time, giddy and goofy with the incredible achievement. Jake was making his dreams real—didn't that make him magical? Who else cared as much as he did? She'd never doubted him. Meanwhile, Jake didn't move. His strong body was limp as he started to speak. Lionel had given him the green light to start when he wanted, so he would ramp up next week in New York.

"Where should we live?" she asked, breathless.

He paused.

"I don't know if it makes sense for us to live together."

"What?"

"I'm going to be working all the time."

Her tone was still upbeat.

"But if we don't live together," she went on, "then I'll never see you."

Jake kept his arms around Sophie.

The truth was, he would break up with her after they graduated next week. He couldn't do it any sooner. Here, at their place, they saw each other so intimately every day, a breakup would be impossible to maintain. Besides, their home in Berkeley was too powerful to destroy. They'd grown too close here to reverse the momentum. This place would always be theirs.

"It wouldn't be fair. I'll get home in the middle of the night, then work more, read. If I'm really in my head, I won't notice if I'm lumbering around. Then, I'll leave early." It was all true, but it wasn't the whole truth. "You deserve better than that."

"You're serious, aren't you?"

He nodded.

"I'm sorry, I won't do that to you."

Sophie was blindsided. With her arms still around his neck, she tried to wrap her mind around this idea that they'd be apart. Did he really believe they'd stay away from each other? Even if they paid two rents, she imagined she'd sleep over at his place, he at hers. They'd keep clothes in each other's closets, leave a toothbrush by the sink. They were only home when they were together. He was her safe haven from everyone else. Meanwhile, Jake said nothing. He seemed staunchly committed to this—and she trusted him.

"This is a phase?" she clarified.

His gut hurt.

"Yes."

"We'll live together when work settles down?"

"Yes."

Eventually, she nodded okay.

"I'm sorry," he said.

"I know."

Jake named his fund Olympus Capital after the mountain on Mars.

Sophie found a studio in Brooklyn.

They texted plans to meet.

That night, in late May, Jake wouldn't be free until 9 p.m. He planned to work after, too, so they'd meet near his office. It was Tuesday. Sophie ate dinner at home in Williamsburg over a copy of *The Ocean at the End of the Lane*, another urban fantasy. She brushed her teeth before taking the subway back into Manhattan, up to 23rd Street, excited. They hadn't seen each other since graduation, when he'd seemed sadder than she'd expected. He'd kept staring at her through the yellow tassel hanging off his graduation cap—over-nostalgic, uncharacteristically teary—when he was supposed to look at Isabel's phone for pictures.

She headed to Madison Square Park. The sky was black but the city illuminated, as if someone had stolen all of the stars and piled them inside the skyscrapers. She sat on a park bench on time and looked up twenty floors to Jake's row of windows. She used to be in tune with what he was feeling. Thankfully, this was just a phase. He'd work around the clock for now, setting up his business, and then they'd find time to share. When Jake exited the building, she smiled. He jogged across the street between two waves of cars.

Sophie stood.

They hugged.

"Hey," he said.

"Hi!"

They sat on the bench with space between them.

Sophie scooched toward him.

"How are you?" she asked eagerly.

"I'm okay."

For the first time since they'd met, Sophie didn't believe him. He wrung his hands hard. He looked pale—he was never pale. For someone living his dream, he looked oddly pinched. She reached out to cup one side of his face. He leaned back.

"I think we should go on a break," he said.

"What?"

"I've been thinking about this for a while. I'm sorry, Sophie. You give too much of yourself up when you're with me. You care too much about us." His pace was slow, his words deliberate. "I keep thinking about you the day we met. I know we want to be together, but the cost to you is too high. I won't take your dreams away."

Dead silence.

"And this isn't even the issue, but the fact is we won't see each other."

"We would if we lived together."

Jake loved her clarity. He ignored the temptation to agree and instead just looked at her. He'd been taking her in like this for weeks, knowing tonight would come. Her tee had a small pom-pom on the front like a rabbit's tail. She'd had that shirt since freshman year. By now, the fluff had been washed out, reduced to wisps.

"For how long?" she asked.

"I don't know."

"Are you *asking* for a break or are you *demanding* one?"

"What?"

"Because if you're *asking*, I say *no*."

He said nothing.

"What does a break even mean?" she pressed.

"That we're not together anymore."

Sophie started to cry.

"I'm sorry. I don't see another way." He wrung his hands harder, pushing a patch of skin to limit of its elasticity. "Do you see how much time you'll have for yourself now, though? Everything you wanted to do—things you still want, I know it—you can. This is a critical period for you, too. Now's the time to set up the rest of our lives."

"Why are you deciding what's right for me?"

"Because I know you."

"Apparently not."

"Sophie. I'm thinking about *you*."

You. Sophie fixated on that word. Her mom had said it too when they talked about Jake senior year. *"You can't force people to love you . . . You can only control yourself."* But Sophie hadn't thought of herself as separate from Jake since freshman year. Since then, he'd mixed with her. He was in all of her habits, likes, the people she knew, in her idea of self. She'd always assumed they'd stay together. *You?* Who was she alone?

Jake explained his decision in different ways.

His choice stayed the same.

Eventually, she accepted it.

"Okay, a break."

She conceded.

"I love you," she added. She must've had a second throat, because those words came from somewhere deeper than her lungs.

They stood up.

They hugged.

Sophie kissed his cheek.

She walked back to the subway.

A break?

Sophie cried over the sidewalk running under her in gray scale. She was surrounded by people in one of the biggest cities in the world, but no one else in the crowd was *her* people. She and Jake hadn't just been dating. He was family. Were they on a break from being family? How could this be happening when she still felt their love? He hadn't responded to her on the bench, but he hadn't needed to. She knew how he felt.

Meanwhile, Jake stood in the lobby with his phone in hand, his last connection to her. Should he text something? Nothing felt big enough. Besides, he wasn't going to change his mind. He pocketed the cold thing and stepped through a turnstile into an elevator. His stomach brewed something horrible. Sophie had taught him about that. In the gut, called the "second brain," there were more nerve cells than in the head. *"And you know, I can talk about this, the biology, everything,"* she said one night in bed. *"But that's not what it's all about it. We're billions of cells, and millions of processes, but we're not that hard to understand. I think at the end of the day, we all just want connection to know we're not alone."* He saw their future home as if it were real, or possible, with her reading in the library. In reality, he stepped out of the elevator toward Olympus and decided the best thing to do was work.

CHAPTER 9

One year later to the day, Sophie walked to Madison Square Park at dawn. The streets were empty minus a runner, then a dog walker branching into three pugs. Parallel lines in the sidewalk converged ahead in an illusion of distance. Traffic lights flashed for no one.

She still couldn't sleep well. After a whole year. In the park, she sat alone on the bench where it had happened. She sensed him with her, a stronger version of what she felt every day. Did people leave pieces of themselves everywhere they went? Morning lightened the air to blue. Eventually, she pulled her phone out of her parka pocket, went to "The Classics," and played Ray Charles's "Georgia on My Mind" at the bottom of the queue. Its time stamp showed he'd added this song just days ago.

Sophie played it again. Was it a happy song or a sad one? Was it the most wistful melody ever composed or was that her projecting? Maybe Jake had added it for her, thinking of her. Maybe *she* was his Georgia, the home that stayed on his mind. The possibility felt like medicine as she held the soft part of her belly below her ribs. She missed her Georgia, too.

"How are you, Sophie?" Dr. Alice White asked the next day, a long month into their sessions. Sophie had barely spoken since they met, but she appeared to *want* to. Every week, she arrived on time and sat by the sofa arm closest to Dr. White's chair. She'd bring her eyebrows together sadly, abruptly. She'd rest two fingers on her lips, then drop her hand to her throat, clearly focused on her own voice and yet not using it. Dr. White kept trying, in front of her Harvard psychiatry degree on the wall, to tease out the knot inside her.

Silence.

"What's on your mind?" Dr. White asked.

Sophie tugged a drawstring on her black Nike hoodie. She wasn't trying to be difficult. She wanted to figure herself out, too. The flashbacks she kept having of Jake were interrupting her daily life. These didn't feel like normal memories. They hijacked all five of her senses. One second, she'd be on the subway to work, dense air plugging her nose, and the next, she was sitting next to Jake in the dining hall, breathing him in again. It was like a lucid dream, but with body, substance, and spectacular detail. She could count the Cheerios in his bowl. She could feel the sun through Berkeley's windows. She was *there*—but so briefly, and without ever losing track of the present—it was as if she were in both moments at once.

Her parents had already sent her to a general physician to see if anything was physically wrong. They wanted to understand not only the "hallucinations"—their word—but her weight loss, pallor, and why her hand kept drifting to her stomach. Sophie kept cradling her belly as if she were alerting the world to a tapeworm. All tests came back healthy.

"Last time, you mentioned 'soul mates'—"

"I said I was reading about them," Sophie corrected.

She'd been reading poems during the day at Free People, looking for other accounts of what she was going through. Rumi had written, "Goodbyes are only for those who love with their eyes. Because for those who love with heart and soul there is no such thing as separation." That passage had felt like a clue. What did psychiatry have to add? Why was she being catapulted into the past, somehow straddling *then* and *now*?

"Right," Dr. White said. "Then you asked me if I believe in soul mates."

"Yes."

"I said there was no evidence of them, and I wanted to say more about that. 'The One,' 'true love'—I went through the literature again." Dr. White leaned forward but spoke gently, afraid to scare Sophie's voice away. "Studies show that people who believe in soul mates are actually more likely to break up and have difficult relationships. Because they believe there's only one person for them, they keep asking themselves: Is this him? Is this 'the One'? A better strategy is to ask, How can I make my relationship better? People are happier when they feel empowered to improve their relationship. When they have a growth mindset, not a destiny mindset."

"I don't think the idea of soul mates hurts people."

"Hm."

She tried to lure more out of Sophie.

The pause snowballed.

"Well," Dr. White conceded, "the idea of soul mates can make it harder for people to move on if they think they found the One." Dr. White's eyes widened as she understood. "What can complicate a breakup further is introversion," Dr. White went on cautiously. "Introverts take more time than others to let their guards down. Then, in an intimate relationship, the introvert is no longer alone. She finds companionship, passion, depth, and trust. When that relationship ends, she—or he, excuse me—may not have close friends to rely on in the transition. She may lack the emotional support she needs, because she had fewer relationships to begin with."

Sophie pinched a tent on the knee of her baggy jeans.

"Why are we talking about this, Sophie?" Dr. White asked.

"He . . ." Sophie's voice cracked. "We were together for four years." Dr. White did not take notes or disturb the momentum in any way. "He asked for a break. I haven't heard from him since then. I don't know, a year ago." *Plus one day.* "We're not together, but . . . I know that we are. There's no evidence of it. I know that. If we went through all the facts together,

I'd agree with you on every one. I don't know how to measure what I'm talking about. I just know we're together. Not in a parallel reality, but in this one. Not in a visible way, but in a real way. I don't know how to prove it yet, but he's with me. I just know."

"You feel like he's with you," Dr. White repeated.

"Yes. Why is that?"

She waited for her answer.

Dr. White held her pen.

"He's in everything I like: places, songs. Why I'm in New York City. I can't see myself without him and—I have these flashbacks of being with him in college. But they're so real." Sophie rubbed her fingers together at eye level, emphasizing how tactile the visions were. "I get transported into these moments with him as if they're happening again, or as if they never stopped happening. I'm in both places at once. I don't understand."

"Breakups can be traumatic."

Sophie flinched.

"I mean *breaks* can be," Dr. White corrected.

"What's happening to me?"

"Studies show the shock can be physical . . ."

Breaths pumped Sophie's chest irregularly.

Dr. White listed the symptoms of a depressive episode.

"In order to live a healthy life again, the first step is to want to. Moving on really is a choice. Studies show it's not only possible to find love again, but common . . ."

Sophie swallowed her disagreement. She wasn't trying to *feel* okay. She was trying to understand. She needed to talk about this with someone who was looking for answers, not someone who thought she had them. What Sophie was sensing had never been explained.

"What is it?" Dr. White asked.

"Nothing," Sophie lied.

Dr. White tapped her pen on her legal pad.

"Sophie," she tried again. "What is it?"

Sophie wiped her eyes.

"I'm sorry. I shouldn't be here."

"Do you want help?"

Sophie shielded her brow, revealing short nails bitten to stubs. Her pinky nail had split in half, divided by a thread-thin line of blood.

"Sophie, are you hurting yourself?"

Sophie hid her hand. She knew Dr. White would have to report any serious self-harm, making the question feel like a checklist item. For the first time since freshman fall, Sophie wished she were talking to Professor Malchik. *He* didn't tick items off by rote. He was the only person she'd ever met who seemed to crave new paradigms and *un*learning, as if those discoveries fed his soul. The stranger her theories were, the better.

"Sophie?" Dr. White said.

Sophie covered her eyes.

"Sophie, will you let me help you move on?"

No. Sophie touched her belly. Her pain was information. She just needed to understand, but maybe that wasn't going to happen here. She looked around the room. The thin floor lamp by her end of the sofa supported a bowl of measly light. It barely lit the box of tissues on the coffee table next to two hardcovers in a row: *Parenting a Prodigy* by Dr. Alice White, MD, and *Inside the Mind of a Gifted Child* by Dr. Alice White, MD. Answers, answers, answers.

Sophie stood.

"Sophie—"

"I'm sorry, but I have to go."

As Sophie rode the subway home, she thought about how she might reach out to Professor Malchik. They were four silent years apart. Their only real time together was marked by her withdrawal: she disappeared pigment by pigment until her lack of interest in his lessons was clear. She needed to do more of her own work before calling on him again. She needed to prove that she was committed to solving this problem, that this wasn't an impulse but was instead connected to something reliable and enduring.

Meanwhile, sitting in front of her, a toddler played with a toy shaped like a segmented green worm. He bent and twisted it into different curves, riveted by the stop motion. The scene lingered with her as she got off at her stop.

Maybe that was the start of an idea.

CHAPTER 10

Peter gripped the podium facing an empty lecture hall. He'd covered a half mile inching side to side. This was the moment he'd been waiting for, ever since he got Sophie's email—Subj: Physics PhD—which had revealed she'd matriculate today.

Apparently, she had a new idea to discuss and would join his Time Theory lecture this fall. She "looked forward to" seeing him in class. He'd googled her right away. In the four years since she'd graduated, she'd only managed inventory at Free People. But what had she been thinking? Einstein had worked a job far below his abilities, too, as a patent clerk while developing his theory of relativity. Had monotony freed her mind? To what end? Peter had spent the past week alert to people around him, looking for her in every face. The new school year was just days old and, for once, he felt the budding energy of it.

His head jerked up when the first student drifted in—not her. Would he recognize her?

And then—

Sophie?

Her bony cheeks tapered into a sharp chin. Her hair was thinner, limper. She was always pale, but now, she verged on translucent under her hoodie.

Meanwhile, Sophie felt unusually vulnerable in this life-size replica of her past. Yale hadn't changed. Their old college—Berkeley—still took up half a city block. Sterling Library was ornamented like a cathedral, as always. Silliman's dining hall featured the same long tables under high ceilings. And—she and Jake had taken a class in this room. Two dozen rows of seats still faced the stage. Retractable desks still separated chairs.

This had been her world at eighteen years old.

Professor Malchik looked just like she remembered: thin, antsy. She waved and sat next to the wall. As she opened her spiral-bound notebook, in a sweeping flashback, she turned an identical cover eight years ago in that room. Jake was with her, right next to her, typing notes on his MacBook. She turned to face him. His dark eyelashes were distinct, countable. He smelled aggressively clean, hard-scrubbed. She felt that moment happening *now*—and, for a heartbeat, she was euphoric—until it slipped away.

She breathed deeply.

She dated a page corner *Sep. 1* in curly script.

"My name is Peter Malchik," Professor Malchik addressed the class. He glanced at his notes on the podium, crestfallen. He'd crafted this introduction for *her*, excited by her reborn, phoenix-like energy. Seeing her in person was deflating—until she raised her gaze to meet his. Her blue eyes were sharp. In them, he saw a sense of purpose not apparent in her body.

"Before our first lecture," he went on as planned, "I'd like to say why I study what I do when the world presents infinite options. The truth is, the world confuses me. Maybe if life were easier to understand, or if I were enamored with vacuous consumerism, I would've gone into another field. But I always felt that 'the world is much richer than what we see.'" It was a quote from Sophie's college essay. "We can't sense everything ourselves, but physics can help us go beyond the reach of what we're given. I encourage you to keep an open mind. What you think is true may be false. What you think is false may be true. My job is to show you what the field believes today. I dare you to improve upon it."

After class, Peter gazed at the steel-wool-like rug, granting his students the comfort of anonymity as they left. He and Sophie had never chosen a time to meet. In their emails—her call, his response—they'd only gone so far as his I look forward to seeing you, too. He peeked to see her walking toward him. Only the two of them remained.

"Hi." Her voice was soft.

"Sophie. Good to see you."

"You too."

His pockets kept him from fidgeting.

Where were the other words?

"I was happy to hear from you." Peter tried to rescue momentum. "And to hear you're back in the field." He studied her from an arm's length away. She had a deep sensitivity to her now—wounded, open—but balanced by new, palpable resolve. "Some PhDs take their time choosing a focus. I was glad to hear you had one."

"Yes. Block theory?"

Oh—*now* it was clear why she wanted his help. Peter had published extensively on that topic. Block theory claimed that all events in the past, present, and future existed at once, frozen in a "block" of space-time. Everything that had happened or would happen was actually occurring *now*. The theory was perfectly captured in Einstein's words, "For us believing physicists, the distinction between past, present, and future is only a stubbornly persistent illusion." This block of space-time was depicted in scientific papers as a 3D rectangle, where the length represented increasing time: at one end lay the big bang, and at the other, the last moment of existence. The block contained, for example, Sophie's birth, every second of her college years, and her death, all at once. Block theory implied that people existed at multiple times simultaneously, but it remained unproven.

"I thought we could talk about it?" Sophie asked.

"I'd love to. And . . . to be clear, you don't need to bring your ideas only to me."

She pinched her eyebrows.

"Anyone would—*will* be happy to help you, whatever you need." He averted his eyes. "You're not obligated to come to me, just because we worked together in the tutorial."

"But I want to talk to you."

"Well, thank you."

"Because you care."

He rapped the side of the podium, energized.

"In that case, we could talk tomorrow?" he asked. The wall clock behind Sophie read 6:10 p.m. He imagined Maggie leaning over a boiling pot of chicken noodle soup in their kitchen. "My wife's expecting me home for dinner soon."

"I could walk you?"

"So, block theory?" Peter probed as they climbed Hillhouse. "How'd you get into that?"

"Intuition."

She felt sheepish admitting that this wasn't a logical quest. It relied on belief without reason and knowing without proof. She imagined these kinds of conversations were typically had with new age healers, pastors, or yoga teachers. How would he react?

"That's okay," he reassured her kindly.

"I became aware that the past isn't gone. It's happening right now."

"You can . . . feel the past?"

"Yes."

"How did this happen?"

"I fell in love." Peter's open mind encouraged her. She let the truth flow. "When you fall in love the way I did, I think your perspective shifts. You're more in touch with the way the world really is. You can see and feel parts of reality you didn't see before."

"I've never heard that," he admitted.

She shrugged.

"When you say 'love,'" he went on, "what does that mean to you?"

"There's an Anish Kapoor sculpture in Maine. It's a metal plate about this big"—she spread her arms to the full length of her wingspan—"and made of mirrors. So, when you stand in front of it, your image is scrambled. You have this sense of being shattered into a million pieces." She and Jake had visited the sculpture at the Colby College Museum of Art in August right before their sophomore year. "To me, love is when you can see someone that way and feel like nothing has changed. It's hard to explain, but when you can scramble their appearance—their atoms, really—and what you feel for them is the same, that's love."

Professor Malchik stopped in front of his house.

"Would you like to come in?" he asked.

She shook her head.

"Please, I insist."

"Sorry, I shouldn't impose. More than I already have."

She tucked a strand of hair behind her ear.

"All right. Well, I'd love to know more. I'll rustle up my old work."

*　　*　　*

Sophie slipped into bed that night wearing the same clothes she'd worn all day. Summer still stuck to the leaves and roasted the pavement outside, but she pulled the covers up to her chin. Lying down made her notice how tense she was. Her back released its web of fists. She turned onto her side and faced the wall. The width of her studio only just exceeded the width of her bed, but she liked that. It felt cozy, like sleeping in someone else's arms. She held her phone and put in earbuds. Nothing new on "The Classics" today. She shuffled her own library, which queued John Mayer's "You're Gonna Live Forever in Me."

Then, Kygo's "Fragile."

Then, The Weepies' "The World Spins Madly On."

The songs washed over her, watering her sadness. Her work had comforted her during the day—she'd felt more energized with every step toward the truth—but now she missed Jake acutely. She could've called her mom for company, but lately, those conversations felt stilted. Sophie didn't have the energy to connect. She resigned herself to falling asleep to songs that understood her, but where was the one person who had?

The next day, in Peter's office, Sophie wore the same hoodie as before. She faced him from the same chair she'd sat in years ago—except this time, she clearly wanted to be here. He'd never seen anyone so determined inside a body so frail. Her hoodie's wide shoulders wilted over her own. But her expression was intent, strong.

Are you okay?

He wanted to ask about her personal life. Then again, her new research was so deeply intimate, by addressing it, he *was* probing the issues closest to her heart.

Peter cleared his throat.

"I haven't stopped thinking about your idea linking love and time. If you're correct, then you might've answered your own thesis question. This doesn't sound at all scientific yet, but it gets us started: the way you see time is to fall in love?" Sophie nodded. "Then, your connection allows you to see beyond your one point in the block."

"Yes."

"Which would explain why you see the past."

She nodded.

"And these aren't memories," she emphasized. "I know I'm in another time. The visions are"—she pinched the air—"thicker. They have smells, temperatures." Jake's warm arm, the snug blanket as they lay in Berkeley's hammock. "Memories have never made me feel hot or cold the way these do. And these are intricate. When you remember a staircase, you can't count the number of stairs in it. Memories are wispy. But when I see the past, I can count everything. I can read the title on every book. The details are there. *I'm* there—and here."

"Have you read . . ." He broached *An Experiment with Time* by J. W. Dunne, a man who claimed to have had prescient dreams about the future. In this book, published in 1927, Dunne listed his dreams and then the subsequent events that they predicted. He proposed the idea that when people were fully conscious, they could only see the here and now. Attention was narrow. It could handle precious little information at once. But when people fell asleep, they slipped into a state that allowed them to see beyond the present. "Dunne never proved anything. My point is, the book has elements of your idea. What if love radically alters perception, the way he suggested sleep did? What if love changes your view as much as dreaming?"

Sophie took notes. As Peter kept indulging his curiosities, she chimed in more and more, thrilling him. After an hour of spirited back-and-forth, they moved to walk around the top of Science Hill, wondering how they might prove something so massive.

New Haven cooled. Blue State Coffee boasted #PUMPKINSZN on its chalkboard in script flecked with orange leaves. Sophie and Professor Malchik talked every day. She stayed late after every Time Theory and walked him home, eliciting dozens of invitations inside: *"Maggie always makes more food than we can eat,"* *"A cup of tea?"* and *"Hot cocoa, maybe?"*

Finally, on the edge of November, she agreed. Professor Malchik led her into the kitchen, where Maggie was stirring a pot of beef stew on the stove. Her kind smile creased every wrinkle. She wore her life happily on her face under a gray-blond bob. Her handshake was eagerly maternal as she wrapped her second hand around Sophie's.

"Welcome, child," she said.

Finally, in person.

Maggie had lived through Peter's high expectations for Sophie almost a decade ago. Then, she'd endured months of his frustration. He'd ask Maggie as much as himself over uneaten dinners, Why was Sophie so distracted? What had he done wrong? Maggie had gone to bed alone for weeks. On her way to their room, she would pass Peter in his study hunched over a problem set he was revising. Now, Sophie was back with passion—and pain.

That night, Maggie watched Sophie, swamped in her clothes, push a chunk of beef around the edge of her bowl. She and Peter speculated about block theory. The discussion was seamless, sharp, but none of the questions Peter asked were the ones Maggie wanted to know. Everything skirted the most glaring topic of all: Sophie's darkness.

Maggie taught special ed in New Haven. Some of her students were brilliant children struggling with emotional issues. Years ago, she had wondered if Sophie was on the spectrum. Did that explain her gifts? Did she have deficiencies that balanced her strengths? Sophie had drifted out of their lives before Maggie had found her answer. Now, Maggie didn't think there was anything deficient about Sophie's ability to feel. This young woman was thoughtful. She listened wholeheartedly and never interrupted Peter. If anything, Sophie was as gifted with empathy as she was with intellect. She was extraordinarily kind—and sad.

"She's grieving," Peter explained that night over the dishes.

"For who?"

Peter shrugged.

"You don't know?"

"Someone she still loves."

"You don't ask her about it?"

"No."

They cleaned in silence.

But if Peter wasn't asking, was anyone?

Sophie became a regular at their dinner table after Time Theory. Their first couple of conversations orbited block theory. Then, Maggie began to interject. She asked Sophie where was she living (*"Right by the 24-hour deli"*) and with whom (*"By myself"*). Maggie backed into information about Sophie's health, family, and the state of her apartment. She cooked heartier foods on the nights Sophie came over: pumpkins stuffed with cheese, pecans, and kale; beef stroganoff with extra-heavy cream; and multilayered cakes with frosting. She hugged Sophie after every evening. She insisted Sophie hang her jacket on the family's rack.

Over time, Maggie learned that Sophie was blindsided by the mention of news events—midterm elections, wildfires in California displacing thousands, and the #MeToo movement—as if she didn't read anything about today. When Sophie asked

Maggie questions about herself, she focused oddly on youth. *"Did you have any pets growing up?"* Maggie had to volunteer facts about their lives now. She told Sophie all about Zack and Benji leading up to their first night home from the University of Connecticut. That fall, they filled the now five seats around the dining room table. Peter had placed a fifth chair next to his, identical to the other four.

Zack and Benji visited a few more times that year. The dynamic they created—talking over each other, erupting into belly laughs, slapping the table—could feel so overwhelming that Sophie escaped to the bathroom during dinner for some peace. There, alone with her phone, she would self-soothe by listening to old voice mails from Jake.

February hung white coats on skeleton trees. Sophie sat across from Peter in his living room while Maggie set the table. Sophie gripped the notebook on her lap. Numbers covered the page so densely, it could have as easily started out black or white.

"Did they help?" Peter asked.

He'd given Sophie her old problem sets to read for inspiration. She'd spent the past few days going through them while logging her thoughts in this journal, her primary companion. She wrote in it during conversations with Professor Malchik; during dinner with his family; and sometimes, she'd stop mid-path on campus in freezing cold to scribble an idea as students parted around her. It was a journalistic approach to her own life.

She didn't want to lose any of the precious wisps in her mind, so delicate and quick to decay that they required immediate recording. They were her key to proving block theory, to showing that time didn't pass the way people experienced it doing so. The past was as real and contemporary as this pen in her hand.

"Sort of," she admitted.

The most interesting part had been a tangent on color. Color, of course, was light, which could be broken down into wavelength and frequency, the number of waves per second. Sophie had written in one page's margin: *Color is a function of frequency. Frequency is a function of time.* On rereading, that note had caught her eye. Since color was visible, and just a mathematical string away from time, she'd thought that the secret to seeing time could be in that relationship. The idea intrigued her again.

The front door swung open to reveal Zack and Benji. Their shaggy hair had snow dandruff. Maggie ran in with oven mitts for hands and hugged them, squeezing the puff out of their parkas. Sophie closed her notebook and waved with her free arm. Peter noted that her grip on the journal stayed tight as everyone said hello. She clung to it like a map she needed to find her way home. Maggie ushered everyone in to dinner: spaghetti and meatballs to power the boys ahead of their ski weekend with friends in Killington, Vermont. Sophie kept the notebook open beside her plate. She poked her plain pasta. She even spun some around her fork at one point, but the spiral failed to hypnotize her. She wasn't interested in food. She mulled over the link between color and time. It connected the visible and the unseen.

She jotted a note every few minutes. The intervals got shorter. She started to write the words between her thoughts—*pause, thinking*—afraid of putting her pen down and missing something vital. She strung whole sentences together with a single line of ink until—

"Sophie, dear," Maggie said.

She twitched and came back to her senses at the table across from Zack and Benji. Both had stalled over their empty plates. Marinara rouged their lips. Behind them, frosted windows blurred the storm outside. Sophie felt Maggie's fingertips on her shoulder and looked down at the pen in her hand, disassociated from own her body. The page was covered in illegible equations. Sophie closed the notebook.

"I'm sorry," she stuttered.

"Are you finished, dear?"

"Yes. I'll get it."

"I have it."

Maggie scooped up the plate, then Peter's, then Benji's. Zack followed her into the kitchen with his own. Sophie looked around for a clue as to what they'd been talking about. Peter excused himself to the restroom. Sophie faced Benji, alone.

"B-r-b," he spelled, getting up.

The kitchen door swung closed behind him.

"What's her deal?" Benji whisper-asked.

Sophie's ears pricked up.

"Shh!" Maggie ordered.

"Cut her a break," Zack said.

"It's fucking weird," Benji whispered.

"She was dumped," Zack said.

"What?" Benji asked.

"Shh, I mean it."

"I thought they were just on the rocks or something," Zack murmured. Sophie's stomach cinched. "I heard him on the phone with her sometimes. Like, in the bathroom. She'd come out and look like she'd been crying. Then I realized they weren't on the phone. I saw her screen. She was listening to old voice mails. From him."

"What a psycho," Benji said.

Sophie stood up and took quick, feather-light footsteps to the front door. She couldn't have made less noise crossing the carpet if she were gliding an inch above the faded pattern. She kept her head bowed as she dressed in her parka, gloves, and boots.

Outside, Hillhouse was dark except for streetlamps. Sophie pulled her iPhone out of her parka pocket and went to her voice mail tab, where his name—*Jake :) Kristopher*—was stacked in rows. She didn't want to delete them. She didn't want to move on. How could she? Her flashbacks were as vivid as ever. She couldn't get through a day without being thrown into the past for one more ecstatic breath beside him. She kept appearing in moments she'd forgotten, seeing details beyond her ability to recall. They were together—now. As she walked home, her tears froze in wave-shaped tracks down her face. She unlocked the door to her building, where her studio waited on the second floor. She called her mom.

"Sophie? What is it?"

It had been a week since they had spoken.

"Am I crazy?" Sophie asked.

"What do you mean?"

Sophie locked her door. She sat on her bed in the dark.

"Am I crazy to go on like this?" Sophie hinged forward at the waist and cried through the words. "Everyone else moves on—"

"Sophie, dear, breathe."

"—but I can't. Why am I so different?" Sophie asked.

"Darling, please."

"I always have been."

"No," Isabel insisted. "You're more *aware* than other people, but what you're feeling is the same. That's the way you've always been. Other people feel what you're going through; you just experience it . . . more." Of course, no one ever wanted to move on. No one ever wanted to fall in love again after they gave their heart away to someone who didn't come back. Isabel hadn't wanted to date anyone after Aidan. But few people actually did swear off others the way Sophie staunchly had.

"Thanks, Mom."

"I love you." Isabel hadn't been able to say that in a while, and she missed her girl. Behind her, water cascaded down a stack of dinner dishes in the sink, tier by tier by tier. "You're not crazy. Not even a little bit, I'm afraid."

"I love you, too, Mom."

Sophie eyed her journal.

"I should go," she added. "Work."

Sophie would've liked to keep talking, but if they did, her mom would start asking the wrong questions. If she were spending time outside, if she were making friends. They said good night. After Sophie hung up, she pulled the pen from her pocket, played the latest song on "The Classics," and felt his old soul in the room like a change in temperature.

A little later that night, as she lay in bed, a flashback overtook her. She was suddenly with Jake as he nuzzled into her belly freshman year.

"Another one?" he asked in the dark.

"All right," she said. "Today, I read about how different animals feel time pass at different rates." She kept stroking his head. "The smaller an animal is, the slower time passes for them." He moaned once, happy. "It helps to think about it in terms of flickering light. When a light flashes on and off quickly enough, an animal sees it as a steady stream without pauses in between. Smaller animals have faster visual systems. So, they're able to see light flashing on and off where we would just see a blur of light, which means they effectively see in slow motion. Flies see the world happen seven times more slowly than we do."

Their chests rose and fell in synch.

"Are you asleep?" she asked.

"I'm listening." He kissed her belly.

"Okay," she went on. "People, too. We feel time pass at different rates depending on what's happening around us. When something unusual happens, we feel time slow down. The brain shifts into overdrive. We analyze every detail. Our visual systems work faster. So we see the world in slow motion, just like the fly."

"So, people can feel time stop?"

When it ended, Sophie was alone in her room—in a different moment, but one as real, as current. She just had to keep working to prove it.

Sophie was gripping both sides of the Malchiks' kitchen sink while Peter and Maggie watched her from the doorway. The running faucet misted her hoodie as she stood immobilized in thought. A bottle of Dial soap lay sideways dripping bright orange goo.

Peter felt like this was his fault. Now in the second year of her PhD, she still hadn't set any boundaries. Whenever he emailed her at 1 or 2 a.m. with readings, she'd reply with her thoughts by morning. When an idea came to him in the middle of the day, and he asked her to drop by his office, she'd appear within an hour without fail. She'd been obsessed with the link between color and time for over a year now. It was an inexplicable hunch, she said, that this related to block theory. However, she hadn't made progress in months.

He'd tried to expand her focus. That afternoon, he'd emailed her a new article on black holes, the phenomena created when a star collapsed at the end of its life. Inside, gravity was so strong, nothing to cross its borders escaped. It was well known that increasing gravity slowed time down, and decreasing gravity sped time up. Next to a black hole, the infinite gravity inside slowed time to the point of standing still. Even though objects were destroyed inside, it took an infinite amount of time for that to occur. So planets and stars appeared to stay on the surface of black holes despite plummeting to the center. In that, Peter saw a connection to their work. Here was an instance where time flowed but had the appearance of standing still. It was the reverse of block theory. Could he and Sophie use the math in that paper for their purposes?

As he stared, Peter regretted sending her that email. She needed more care, not more to read. It was time to address her personal life directly. After all, Sophie ate dinner with them every night at home. From a distance, she had the same coloring as Zack and Benji.

He cleared his throat.

Sophie jolted.

"Why don't we go to my study," he suggested.

Sophie grabbed her notebook—its weathered pages stacked in waves—and followed. Upstairs, they passed Zack's and Benji's empty rooms on their way to the end of the hall. In Peter's study, bookcases replaced wallpaper. Every shelf had more books than room for them. Hard- and softcovers stuffed the space above rows stacked two deep and stood in tall piles on the floor. Peter sat in an armchair with a soft, tasseled blanket hanging over the arm. He offered Sophie its twin facing him. He looked uncomfortable despite plush back cushions. Sophie shut the door behind them and sat with caution. Peter tented his fingertips.

"I've known you now, awhile?" he began.

She nodded.

"From day one of your first year in college. And here we are, in your second year as a PhD." He bounced his fingertips off each other, thinking there was only one way to help her. If it compromised their work, so be it. "Maggie is so fond of you. As are Zack and Benji. They don't show it as much, but they care. We always want you to feel welcome here."

"I do."

"I think now's a good time to tell you a bit more about myself." He decided to ease into it. "Part of the reason why Maggie and I clicked was timing. Part of it was we both cared about our work, and I loved how kind she was. People without strong personalities can get described as 'nice' in the filler sense of the word, meaning they have no notable qualities whatsoever. But Maggie is remarkably, proactively *nice* in a way I never was and always admired. Most important, she and I always had the same idea of family. For better or worse, we wanted to stick together and create our own. Some people have that in them. Some don't. We consider you part of our family. You always have another home with us."

"Thank you."

"Of course." He paused. "Maggie and I've been together almost our whole lives, but we waited a while to have children. When she got pregnant, we were in our thirties. It was a very special time for us. We'd imagined having children together for so long. We had the boys. We'd always wanted three. When she got pregnant again, we were going to have a girl. I think she still has the clothes." He wrung his hands. "She was older by then. The doctors always said losing her was a possibility. For some reason, we always imagined three."

He cleared his throat.

"I haven't talked about this in years," he said.

"I'm sorry."

"The boys don't know, either. I'm telling you this to say I know what it's like to lose someone special, irreplaceable. We have two sons, but they don't replace Annie. I've learned there's no getting over, but there is moving on. There is life after loss. It's not the same, and you always remember, but it doesn't have to hold you back. I'm not trying to intrude. You don't have to tell me anything. I only know what I see in you. And I recognize it."

In grief, as he well knew, time appeared to stop. The rest of the world kept going and growing, but grievers didn't. They were locked in the past as they revisited old photos, mementos, and memories, asking themselves if they'd really done everything they could. They struggled with everything they'd never do again with the one they lost. It was like being frozen on the edge of a black hole—or experiencing block theory—and the signs were all over Sophie. She looked the same way she had when she stepped foot into Time Theory. Peter wondered if she was wearing the same hoodie, if that hoodie was *his*.

"I know what it looks like," she said. "But I didn't lose him."

Peter furrowed his brow.

"I think we're still together. Just . . . not . . ." Sophie moved her hands back and forth as if she were pumping an invisible accordion. It was a motion they'd made before to describe the way a person is spread out in a block of space-time.

"Not . . . right here?" Peter prompted.

"Exactly. Not here, but—"

"Now."

She nodded.

Peter tapped his long fingers with unusual slowness. Her sadness weighed on his jitters. He still knew nothing about the man allegedly sharing the moment with them. He only saw Sophie, how tightly she clung to her journal, how intently she worked, and everything she was sacrificing all these years later to hold onto the idea of them. The fate of block theory and her old relationship were intertwined. If it were true, they really were still together. He really was still with Annie. Maggie and he were still meeting for the first time. There was something desperately sad about Sophie's quest, but something heroic about it, too. He hoped that the love of her life—whoever he was, wherever he was—knew the value of what he'd lost.

"Well," he said at last, "that bastard better deserve it."

*　　*　　*

The next day, Jake eyed his phone in the elevator up to Olympus. His broad shoulders tapered to a slim waist under his tailored suit. He was focused and calm to the point of surgical steadiness until Lionel's name graced his in-box.

> A minute?
> Lionel Padington
> CEO, Padington Associates

Usually, when Lionel wanted to talk—asking questions as one of Jake's investors, or offering advice as his mentor—he just walked across the floor and into Jake's office. The double doors branded PADINGTON ASSOCIATES faced the pair bearing OLYMPUS, its offshoot now managing $52 million. Jake had grown Lionel's seed money over 20 percent every year, and the staggering feat had enticed other pocketbooks. He employed four recent college grads and a twenty-four-year-old with only a high school diploma. All were whip-smart, driven kids who'd been rejected everywhere else for lack of experience. They acted eager to stay on a winning team in the highest paid industry in the world.

A minute?

Yesterday, they'd talked for an hour. Lionel had knocked on Jake's door wanting to know more about his massive new investment in Roxster. In Lionel's view, it was a strange choice for Olympus. Jake had always bet on proven companies that modeled themselves after winners of the past. But Roxster was a small new smartwatch company. It invested so much in research, it didn't turn a profit. Its pipeline of future products was untested. In rebuttal, Jake compared Roxster to Apple and other tech giants, but Lionel didn't appear satisfied. Eventually, Lionel wearied and sipped his cold half-thermos of coffee. Before he left, he mentioned Giulia's birthday party next week and asked Jake if he'd like that plus one. *"No, sir."*

Jake strode through the doors of Padington Associates. He speed-walked by people barking on headsets until a scalding slap on his chest stopped him.

"Fuck!"

Hot coffee dripped down his shirt.

A bespectacled assistant froze with a tray of Starbucks cups.

"I'm *so* sorry, Jake."

"I shouldn't yell. It's my fault."

The assistant dabbed at his shirt with a brown napkin.

"Please, don't worry about it," Jake said.

"Hi, Jake," two young men in Padington vests said as they passed. Jake didn't hear them. He took another napkin from the tray and joined her in drying his shirt. He tried to tell her it was all right. When she finished fretting over him, he made his way to Lionel's corner office, knocked on the open door. Lionel stood by the window with one hand in his pocket. He seemed less animated than usual as he waved Jake in and stared at the brown blotch on his shirt. Lionel sat at his desk and offered Jake the chair across from him.

"I wanted to have a talk," Lionel said slowly.

"Is everything okay?"

Lionel rested one hand, his wrist limp, on a stack of papers in front of him.

"Yesterday, I asked you about a plus one to Giulia's party. It's a minor detail—whether or not you bring anyone—but it got me thinking. About how hard you work. How much time you spend here." Lionel paused. "Are you happy?"

His eyes squinted doubtfully.

"Yes, of course."

Lionel grunted.

"I won't say this again, son. If you're not happy, it isn't worth it."

"I'm happy!" The words came back at Lionel so quickly after his advice that they sounded reflexive, not a product of any introspection.

"Do me a favor. Go do something for yourself."

"Yes, of course."

"No," Lionel snapped. He recovered himself. "Think about it. For a second. Digest what I'm saying. How old are you now?"

Jake paused.

"I am twenty-eight." Jake left space between each word.

"Are you seeing anyone?" Jake hadn't mentioned a woman's name since Sophie Jones in college. With the hours he logged in the office, Lionel doubted the boy had sat down for a face-to-face date in years. As the silence stretched, Lionel became convinced not only that the answer was no, but that answers to derivative and related questions were no: no upcoming dates, no thoughts of them, no intention of them, and no plain vanilla guy friends in the mix, either, relationships that required only a beer every few months to maintain. "Okay, don't answer that. But think about it. Think about who'll be at your finish line. If no one comes to mind, you won't make it. It won't be worth it. You need other people, or at least to enjoy yourself more. I know you're gifted, but you're a human being. You can't double down on work forever. That's not success, and it's not sustainable. Things that aren't balanced fall down."

Jake collected himself. Lionel had never intervened in his personal life. Their bond had been forged over their shared identity as self-starters and relentless workers. For Lionel to step in and tell Jake to relax—maybe he had gone off the deep end. As Jake let the pause be, though, he didn't feel criticized as much as he felt cared for. Lionel was looking out for him.

Lionel's expression softened as Jake wrestled with the advice. He was a stellar kid—imperfect, outstanding. On the floor, his nickname was Einstein. The boy was too intimidating for people to say it to his face, so it stayed behind-the-back. Yes, Jake posted genius results, and Einstein was a genius. But Einstein was also famous for disarray: messy hair, a cluttered desk. He never wore socks. He never learned his own phone number. In a similar way, Jake didn't see people standing right in front of him. He sometimes asked his assistant if he'd eaten lunch. He never remembered what day of the week it was. At first, Lionel had found it amusing. Then endearing when he realized that

Jake's strength—allowing him to channel all of his energy into one lane of life at a time—was a vulnerability, too. Jake might not have noticed his lack of personal life. Everyone needed help now and then.

"If you want to talk more—about anything—I'll be here."

"Thank you."

"Course, son."

Lionel shooed him away, overly dismissive to correct for the intimacy. After Jake left, Lionel stared ahead at the photo of them shaking hands by the Olympus doors. Lionel liked how similar they looked in that shot, like the same person thirty years apart. That had been taken on Jake's first morning in the new office. Had the boy stopped working since then? His dedication was supernatural, sure, but the most unusual thing about Jake's work ethic was that it had soul. He loved what he did. It wasn't right for someone with spirit like that to be alone. Lionel never had found out what had happened between Jake and Sophie. He figured that girl must've broken Jake's heart from the way he moped around for months after.

Jake strode back into Olympus. His analysts sat in an open floor plan with Tawny, his assistant, a single mom Janice's age. Everyone turned an inch toward him as he passed. He stayed in his own mental tunnel. In his office, he sat in the black chair he'd saved from his dorm room office in college. *Enjoy yourself more.* How was he supposed to do that?

*　　*　　*

Jake trailed the realtor's high-heeled strut into a $60k-per-month penthouse two weeks later. His only free time that week had come at 10:15 p.m. on a Saturday night. They were alone in the apartment. Beyond her—Stacy? Was that her name?—sleek brown hair, which reflected every chandelier here, floor-to-ceiling windows framed a panoramic view of New York City. Manhattan looked like his own personal backyard. Jake nodded, impressed.

"Is it big enough?" Stacy asked.

She arched a thin eyebrow. Jake had the distinct impression she was flirting with him. As she gave him the brochure, her red nails grazed his palm. They began the tour. Every one of the three bedrooms had a walk-in closet and terrace. The building had a seventy-foot saltwater pool next to bocce courts, as well as a golf simulator. He'd have access to a chauffeured Lexus at any time. He nodded. At least Stacy moved quickly. The last tour he'd endured had been led by a man who'd gone into excruciating detail about the "rustic yet glamorous" trellis pattern on the walls. This handful of tours was the most social he'd been in months, maybe years. So far, the only thing they'd accomplished was to remind Jake he didn't get along with most people.

"Do you have kids?" she asked.

"No. Why?"

"This building has great perks for kids. Now, the best for last." Stacy handed Jake one of two bubbling champagne flutes on a table beside double doors. She took the other for herself. *Clink.* She pushed the door open to reveal a king bed under a skylight of the same size. "*This* is my favorite part." She pointed up. "It's the best view in the whole city." Her tight pencil skirt allowed only small steps as she moved to the corner. When she turned off the lights, she turned *on* emphasis to the sky. The dark view was almost starless, barely freckled with white.

"See?" she said. "There's one."

Jake looked at the pinprick she referenced.

"That's not a star," he said.

"Hm?"

"That's Venus," he said. "It's a planet."

"Planet, star." She treated them as synonyms.

"They're different."

Jake and Sophie lay in their bed sophomore winter. Outside their window, the Milky Way glittered. Sophie pointed at two radiant orbs and identified Venus next to Uranus. Both glowed next to Pisces, the V shape she'd already taught him. Jake tried to memorize the scene. She crooked her leg across him under a blanket up to their chins.

"Do a moon one," Jake said.

On command, Sophie pointed to Jupiter and its four moons. She named the space lab when it whizzed by like a cosmic firefly.

"Do you ever run out of things to teach me?" he asked.

She laughed.

"Are you ever just like, 'Shit shit shit what now?'"

"Not really."

She kissed his cheek.

"Can you see the markings on the moon?" she asked.

"You're so beautiful."

"The shadows?" she prompted.

"Oh." He looked out the window again. "Yeah."

"The moon doesn't have an atmosphere. That means no air. No wind. So, everything on the moon—all the craters, astronaut boot prints, everything—will always be there. There's no water to wash it away. Whatever marks are up there will be there a million years from now." Meanwhile, Jake brought her hand to his mouth. He pressed her fingertips to his lips in a slow kiss. "But I like that. On Earth, life cycles are so short. Down here, everything's always changing and decaying. In space, it's different. If you touch two pieces of metal together in the vacuum, they fuse together forever. After that, you can't break them apart."

He kissed the top of her head.

"Another one?" he asked.

"All right," she said.

She nestled in his arms.

"So, everything in the universe is made of atoms, right?" she started. He nodded, nuzzling his chin up and down against the side of her head. "Inside every atom, there's a nucleus surrounded by electrons in clouds. These clouds aren't that close to nucleus. There's a lot of empty space . . ." She *trailed off.* *"What I'm saying is, we think of the world as* *solid, but most of it isn't. Almost all matter—more than 99.9* *percent of it—is empty space. If you took all that space out of* *our atoms, the entire human race would fit into the volume* *of a sugar cube."*

"I believe it."

"Well, good. It's true."

He laughed.

"I just meant that when you think about people, the things *that stand out about them aren't what you can see and touch,* *right?" he said. "Does that make sense? I don't know. There's a* *lot more to you than just what I see."*

It was the longest flashback he'd ever had. When it ended, he still felt her with him. Her presence was in the master bedroom, inside him, everywhere.

It hadn't gotten any easier for him to deal with the visions. They were all-consuming and packed with details he'd forgotten, down to the specific spray of stars, the spearmint toothpaste on his tongue, and how free it felt to be that young again, in the thick of the greatest luxury on earth: time with the one he loved.

He'd never told anyone about his episodes. No one would believe him. The difference between *remembering* a moment and *being in it* was instantly felt, impossible to convey. But he knew. When a flashback hit, he just knew he was in that moment as much as he was here now. It had occurred to him that maybe he'd left so much of his heart in those times with Sophie, he had to rotate among them as a way to stay whole. He'd spread himself out, and the flashbacks held him together. Of course, that didn't make sense, but he accepted the idea like a spiritual truth irreconcilable with fact. He missed her every day.

"I'll think about it," Jake lied.

He checked his watch.

"Would you like to see—" Stacy began.

"Sorry, I have to get on a call. Great to meet you, Stacy."

"Tracy."

"What?"

"My name."

"Oh." He'd imagined the S? "Sorry. Thank you again."

On the street, the city was dark and bright at once. Light was confined to windows, headlights, and traffic lanterns. Their auras were stark, and beyond them, shadow. Jake headed for the subway home. He'd lived in the same studio since graduating and renewed the lease every May. After all, he didn't spend much time there. He didn't have people over. Did he really need more space? But here he was, "enjoying" himself. He made a mental note to email Tracy *no* and take the next apartment without a tour. His only request: no skylights.

He stopped at the station, looked up at the sky. Where was she right now? He knew she was getting her PhD at Yale because he googled her every few weeks. He'd been thrilled to see that change to her LinkedIn two years ago. He *had* made the right decision. Her profile picture was still the same thumbnail she'd had when they graduated. Did she look different? What was she working on? Was she seeing anyone?

He imagined what they'd do if they passed each other tonight. It was a fantasy he usually indulged in the mornings on his way to work. Now, he pictured her walking toward him. Her hair was still long, her eyes still hot blue. She held a library book in plastic casing. Then what? In one scenario, they both kept walking to steer clear of the wound. In another, they stopped and stumbled through inadequate conversation, listing basic facts about their lives. Butterflies lifted not just his stomach but his arms, throat, and chest. That would precede the agony of remaking his decision to pull away. In another daydream, they continued unquestioningly into each other's arms. He apologized with his first breath and never let her go.

But those were fantasies.

He checked the time on his watch, a Roxster prototype he'd put on for the first time this morning. Its sleek black bangle combined his phone, computer, credit card, health records, doctor—everything—and would be on the market next year.

He hadn't told Lionel the whole truth about Roxster. The truth was he'd been reading about the company weeks ago when he'd spotted an unusual footer in its investor presentation. The company had disclosed that it funded academic research on time. Jake had requested a meeting with the company's CEO, Steve Traffy. Steve turned out to be a short man with a tall personality: hyperverbal, quick to laugh. After some get-to-know-yous, Jake had asked Steve about the unusual disclosure. Apparently, Roxster co-funded programs at a few Ivy League schools studying the nature of time itself. Jake realized that by investing in Roxster, he was investing in Sophie's field. He could help her. So he made Roxster his flagship name.

Jake stepped onto the subway with Sophie in his heart. Of course, he'd never stop trying to help her. But some things, she had to give herself.

CHAPTER 11

After years of failing to prove block theory, Sophie changed her focus in order to graduate. She wrote her dissertation on chromesthesia, a type of synesthesia. For people with this condition, sounds had color. Hearing music made them see vibrant, dynamic abstractions. It reminded Sophie of her flashbacks. When she had to justify the topic to the chair, she framed it as research on converting one kind of sensory input to another: sound to sight. Similar studies had laid the groundwork for infrared imaging, which converted heat to sight.

As part of Sophie's work, she explored the onset of chromesthesia. Most people with the ability to "see" music were born with it. However, it was possible to develop the sense. She interviewed a hundred adults who had. In her long list of questions, at the bottom—belying its importance to her—she included *Do you believe in soul mates?* A staggering

90 percent of the chromesthetes did. Sophie always posed the natural follow-up: *Have you met yours?* If so, when? Everyone she asked had developed chromesthesia *after* meeting their soul mate.

Sophie did not mention that in her dissertation. She only showed Peter what she found. It spoke to their hunch: something about falling in love radically altered perception.

"Zack!" Sophie called confidently. He stood a head taller than most of the runners by the start line. He jogged toward her with Benji.

"You ready?" Zack asked.

"As ready as you two," she quipped.

Zack smirked.

She'd agreed months ago to race with them in the New Haven Half Marathon. Now, in the final weeks of her PhD, days before her thirty-second birthday, it was here. She hadn't run more than three miles at a time in years. She'd spent most of her life sitting down, and this semester, thinking had confined her even more than usual as she finished her dissertation. She lost her breath sometimes on the walk up Science Hill, but she'd finally agreed to the race. It was a "Malchik tradition," according to Zack, "for the kids."

Her high ponytail was secured with a rubber band she'd taken from her desk half an hour ago. Zack and Benji wore matching sweatbands from their fraternity. Peter and Maggie stood nearby, ready with camera phones. Sophie was swinging her arms back and forth when a loudspeaker ordered their heat to take their marks. Benji touched his toes over bent knees, looking like the leftmost primate in an evolutionary time lapse. The race gun fired. Benji sprinted ahead. Zack disappeared after into the fray of billowing apparel as Sophie leaned into a jog. More and more people passed until she found herself in step with an older crowd.

The route was shaped like a figure eight. She walked miles three, five, and six but never stopped. Leafy trees cast jagged shadows on the asphalt. She drank Dixie cups of water from folding tables. The spectating mob thickened and thinned. As she jogged back through the heart of campus, right at the junction of the 8, setting a new personal record with each step, she ran by the psychology building where she and Jake had met. *They stood three steps apart, their bodies connected by light.* The flashback energized her. Her cadence picked up again when she passed Silliman's dining hall where they first ate together. *They froze in a wishbone angle joined at the mouth.*

Sophie ran beyond the invisible edge of campus. Panting dried the back of her throat. Midday sun bore down on her red face. A sign informed her that she had 3.1 miles to go. She reminded herself that the Malchiks were at the finish line. She pictured them hugging Zack and Benji congratulations. Maybe Maggie was tearing up between her sons in a group photo. Or maybe Benji was bent over heaving. The boys had never been very athletic aside from this race, which they ran every year to raise money for the school where Maggie worked.

Sophie wished her parents were standing at the finish line, too. Neither of them knew she was running today. She didn't answer their calls often. When she did, she found it hard to talk about herself. She resorted to one-word responses and didn't volunteer any news because she didn't feel like she was making them proud. *"I just want to make sure you aren't taking school too seriously."* And here she was, a PhD, obsessed with a theory. She'd written a different dissertation, but her fixation remained. She'd never let it go.

Now, she imagined her parents waiting for her. Her mom was wearing hoop earrings with dreamcatcher webbing. Her dad had his arm around her. They were accepting half-pints of Poland Spring from the Malchiks in the crowd full of families.

And Jake.

She pictured him off to the side. He kept his MacBook tucked under his arm, looking exactly like he did in college. A Nike tee clung to his chest. She sprinted ahead, passing a couple of runners. Her head felt light. Her feet felt lighter. Jake needed her to finish so they could go home. They didn't have anything in particular to do. Maybe they'd have dinner in Berkeley and talk on the sofa in their double until Sophie couldn't keep her eyes open anymore. He'd help her up. They'd fall asleep in a narrow lane on one side of their bed. Sophie's last feeling would be *home*. When the finish line finally came into view, Sophie didn't stop imagining him. He gazed back with soulful eyes. Peter was pointing her out to the rest of his family as she sprinted under the enormous digital clock marking the end of the race. She skidded to a stop and hinged forward until her head was in line with her waist.

"Well *done!*" Peter congratulated.

She stood up.

Zack's and Benji's medals dangled around their necks.

"Wow," Benji admitted.

Maggie offered Sophie a water. She gulped it down.

"What was her time?" Benji asked.

"A few minutes after you," Zack said.

"Wow," Benji repeated. "Your last mile was like *Transformers.*"

"What'd you say?" Sophie snapped.

"Benji," Maggie chided.

Transformation—that was it. She didn't know why she'd never considered it before.

"I have to go," Sophie said.

"Will you be back for dinner?" Maggie asked.

Sophie walked, ran, and then sprinted, moving faster than everyone else past the finish line until she reached her building. Inside, she jumped up the stairs two at a time. She'd lived in the same studio since she moved back to New Haven. The small box was too sparse to be messy. A gray futon faced her desk between a kitchenette and her bed. Her cupboards stored just two boxes of saltines and a full jar of peanut butter. Her desk was the focal point. She sat down facing a bulletin board covered with Post-it notes and scribbled equations. Stacks of books and journals fanned out in a semicircle behind her.

She reached for a pen.

She opened a fresh notebook.

In one of her thousands of attempts to prove block theory, she'd tried in vain to remove *time* as a variable from a dozen equations of motion. That would prove it didn't matter when events occurred. There was no absolute flow of time. All moments were now—the Fourier transformation. Sophie remembered it from her final problem set freshman year. This operation took equations from the time domain and mapped them onto the frequency domain. It changed the unit from time in seconds to, for example, hertz. Even when she'd reread the problem set years ago, she hadn't understood what it could be. But this technique was the one. This was the piece she'd hunted for almost a decade. The Fourier transformation would convert all of her functions of time into frequencies and thereby remove the *time* variable completely.

This was it.

This was proof.

Equation by equation, Sophie transformed everything into Fourier space. She filled page after page, front and back. She didn't feel like she was doing math. She was telling the world what it had felt like to be her. This was where her intuition had led.

Sophie tugged the dangling string of her desk lamp when daylight faded. She kept working until, finally, deep in the black belly of night, she succeeded in converting every description of motion into one independent of time. She reclined against the straight back of her chair. She'd felt Jake with her for years. She'd seen them together every day. But right then, as she stared at the last page forming incontrovertible proof of block theory, Sophie saw all of him. She saw not just one moment, but all of their time together suspended around her because all of it was happening now. She cried, shaking with tears that wet her fingertips, cheeks, and chin. Jake had been the only one she ever wanted because they had always been and always would be together. Her notebook didn't just prove block theory.

To Sophie, it proved love.

Jake was sitting in his office on the Fourth of July weekend when breaking news dominated his Bloomberg terminal. "Yale PhD Solves Space-Time Mystery." "Yalie Answers: What Is Reality?" "The Discovery of the Century: Block Theory." Jake clicked on an article hoping to see the name Sophie Jones in the lede. And there she was.

Apparently, she'd just spent the past six hours in Cambridge. In its biggest lecture hall, across twenty whiteboards, she'd written every line in her proof of block theory. Jake read a second article, then a third. By all accounts, there hadn't been a doodling hand, bouncing knee, or vacant stare in the room. Sophie had single-handedly riveted the hundreds of physicists, math legends, thought leaders, and spiritual icons in attendance for the entire afternoon. Her proof had ended with a heated Q&A, and then, finally, thunderous applause.

Jake stood to shut the door to his office before he remembered everyone else had fled for the holiday weekend. Every monitor was dark. His Roxster read 10:02 a.m. in lightsaber blue. Back at his desk, he read every new story. The comments section after every article was flooded with opinions. People grappled with how this bore on the big questions in life. If all moments existed at once, did free will exist? Talking heads debated on live-streaming panels about it. A couple of celebrity contrarians denied block theory, but the quants did not. This was the biggest advance in understanding space and time since Einstein's theory of relativity in 1905. Sophie Jones would be written into every high school textbook.

Jake's heart beat faster.

He was ecstatic, proud, victorious.

She'd done it.

A brand new *Daily Mirror* article included a photo of Sophie from that afternoon. He leaned back in his chair as fast as if he'd been shot through the heart. In the picture, Sophie cowered from a flash while walking by smart cars on a cobblestone street. He could only see her profile. Her hair was as bright and as long as he remembered, but thinner and sleek down her back. Was she happy? As happy as she deserved to be?

He spun around to face a view of Madison Square Park. Between trees, he saw where it had happened. The last time he'd spoken to her. He'd been a millimeter from texting her hundreds of times, but it had never felt right. His thumb always hovered over the *send* arrow for just long enough that he came to his senses. They needed to be apart. Why make that more difficult than it had to be?

But now—she'd done it.

She'd made it.

He started planning what to say, how. Texting would be too casual. Calling would be too invasive. He'd email her. For the rest of the afternoon, he picked words from the opening—*Dear Sophie* was too presumptive, just *Sophie* was better—to his signature.

He kept refining it. For the next week, his email was an intensely pleasurable obsession. Even after the news cycle moved away from Sophie, Jake stayed. He wanted his message to be just right. He was combing back through the media storm, searching for last-minute inspiration, when he came across an interview with her taped by the *Yale Daily News*. Its thumbnail showed a triangular *play* button over her profile. *Click.* She looked thinner, but stronger. She didn't shy from her interviewer the way he would've expected her to. She looked right at the camera a few times, with her spirit shining through her eyes. Jake decided to send his email as soon as the video ended. He didn't want to waste more time.

The one-minute clip ended with two startling lines:

"So, what's next for you?" the student reporter asked.

"I have some ideas," Sophie said.

Jake blinked.

He watched it again.

"I have some ideas."

Jake pinched his eyebrows together. When he lifted his head again, he studied the draft on his computer.

Sophie,

Congratulations! I am in awe of your proof.

I could be witty—I hope—but I'd rather be straightforward. The truth is I would love to talk to you again. Not about anything in particular. It's just been too long. I can come to New Haven at any time. If I understand block theory correctly, we are already there now (or not, as you wish), which is a nice thought in the meantime.

Sincerely,

Jake

"I have some ideas."

Letter by letter, he erased his email.

Sophie had taught him in college about the greatest breakthrough of the 1800s: James Maxwell's discovery of electromagnetism. He connected electricity, magnetism, and light in revolutionary equations that enabled some of the most impactful inventions of all time—including Thomas Edison's light bulb. Sophie had told Jake that Maxwell made his biggest intellectual leaps in his thirties, all in a single year.

Sophie was barely thirty-two.

"I have some ideas."

PART TWO

Twenty-Five Years Later

CHAPTER 12

Sophie followed her last two students out of the lecture. Despite her silver hair—barely in its braid, a wild vine down her side— at fifty-six years old, she looked younger than most of her peers teaching at Yale. Her tee had a ring of ladybugs around each sleeve. Fine lines touched her eyes and mouth, especially when she smiled, but her clear skin dazzled.

She walked down Hillhouse enjoying the February afternoon. In her twenty years teaching physics, this street had barely changed. Temperatures had risen, stretching springs and summers, but these were the same evergreens she'd grown up with: white firs and blue Atlas cedars covered with green needles. Yale was still uncannily like her college memories. Classes were still taught as lectures. The school had only grown by three hundred students. Most buildings had been exactly maintained. She was passing the Malchiks' house as usual after Time Theory when a young man crossed the street in front of her. He turned onto Sophie's path a few steps ahead. She stopped short—that profile. The narrow face, sharp chin, dark hair—all suggesting focus. Sophie felt an acidic explosion in her gut. She squinted at the receding back of his head. Those shoulders, right here, were the same ones she'd known in college.

"Do a moon one."

The young man walked beside a lithe Indian woman with long black hair. They held hands loosely. Sophie followed. The couple pushed open the gate toward Silliman. She trailed them into the courtyard, inside Silliman, and then up marble stairs where they disappeared into the dining hall ahead of her. Sophie stood on the threshold. The roaring room verged on capacity. Kids swerved around each other with teetering trays full of food. A bulky man in a Yale Football sweatshirt brushed her shoulder as he passed.

Who had she just seen? He might've been a distant relative or a figment of her imagination. She drifted inside and sat by the window at a long table. She typed "Jake K" on her Roxster for some kind of clue. The fill-ins:

Jake K**ristopher**

Jake K**ristopher net worth**

Jake K**ristopher house**

She tapped his name. His Wikipedia page was the first search result of over three million. As she looked at his photo, she hugged herself with one arm. His short hair was mostly salt, barely pepper. Still, something about knowing people when they were young made them always look that way to you.

"**Jake Kristopher** (born December 1, 1992) is an American billionaire investor and philanthropist. Kristopher is CEO of Olympus Capital, one of the largest hedge funds, now managing more than $105 billion. His net worth is estimated at $10 billion . . ."

But she knew that already. Even though they hadn't spoken in over thirty years, it had been easy to keep up with him. Olympus made the news often for its stellar results. Jake was photographed at charity fundraisers. He appeared on NBC and other channels to give stock picks and his opinion on the macroeconomy. Sophie had seen him on the TV always running on mute in the physics faculty lounge. Success had made him a public figure.

She thought he might've reached out in the days, weeks, or months after she proved block theory. He must've heard about it. And after what they'd shared together—all the vulnerable moments before they'd done anything or were anyone—he must've considered saying something. Then, nothing at all. To her, his lack of contact sent a clear message: he didn't think they should be together. Even though Sophie had proven they still were.

She'd thought about reaching out herself. The trouble was that none of the appropriate things felt honest and nothing honest felt appropriate. They'd never had a light touch with each other. They hadn't been friends first. Even when they'd met, as they alternated questions on their way to lunch, they were already falling in love. Besides, Jake seemed to be thriving. In every interview, he looked sharp as ever, as fit as he was in college. His teeth were straight now. He appeared to be living the future he'd always envisioned.

Sophie scrolled down to Jake's Personal section.

Wooden chair legs screeched.

She lifted her head.

Jake's college double sat down at the end of her table. A sour shock came up her throat and stole her breath. The Indian woman sat next to him. He draped his arm around the back of her chair. He kissed her cheek. A tiny feather floated to land on the floppy collar of his white linen shirt. The woman pinched it with long, elegant fingers and flicked it free. Sophie glanced between the photo of Jake on her watch and the young man in front of her. As the feather from his shirt blew toward her, the couple traced its path to Sophie.

"So, people can feel time stop?"

Sophie kept staring at the lookalike.

He waved, rose, and approached her from across the table. His wide smile was kind. He slid his big hands into khaki pockets. Sunlight danced in his bright eyes.

"Hi," he said.

Sophie felt unhinged.

What was happening?

Who was he?

Her gut was silent and cavernously empty.

She had to speak.

"Sorry," she said.

"Have we met?" he asked.

"No."

"I'm Liam."

He extended his hand in slow motion.

"So, people can feel time stop?"

Liam's hand waited.

"Are you okay?" Liam asked.

"Sorry. It's just."

She shook his hand limply.

He looked worried.

"The resemblance," she stuttered.

"Ah," he said. "So you knew him."

Sophie didn't understand.

"My biological father," Liam explained.

Sophie wrinkled her brow.

"You're Jake's . . ."

"Son," Liam finished.

He winced.

"I don't say that often." He smiled uncomfortably.

Sophie cleared her throat.

"I didn't know he had . . ."

Any children.

"What's your name?" he asked, friendly.

"Sophie. I teach physics here."

"Oh, I'm taking physics," Liam said. "To graduate. Physics and Society, the easiest class. I'm going to get the tutors' help after lunch. I'm an art major."

He laughed.

"Though I'm not sure the tutors will help," he added doubtfully.

"Why not?"

"I'm at the level *below* being helpable," he said. He stacked his hands one under the other. "I always end up asking them questions about themselves and getting distracted. Then we're getting coffee. I'm showing them pictures of my work. It's a disaster."

Jake never would've gotten distracted like that. The physical resemblance between them was there, but all the intangibles were different. Liam had none of Jake's darkness—and yet, every inch of his face. Sophie didn't want him to leave.

"I'd be happy to take a look," Sophie asserted.

"Oh no," Liam said. "I wouldn't impose."

"I insist."

Sophie was firm.

"Please," she added more kindly.

Liam acquiesced.

He removed a tablet from his backpack and introduced Sophie to Daya, his girlfriend. Daya was also an art major. She had small features: slim nose and thin lips on an almond-shaped face. Her glossy black hair shone.

"You look familiar," Daya announced.

Sophie smiled, left the mystery be. She'd heard versions of that for decades. After all, her proof had generated global buzz. Her identity used to be a popular Halloween costume. A blond wig, notebook covered in handwritten equations and sketched clockfaces, and Yale sweatshirt constituted The Sophie Jones. The outfit was sold in a vacuum-sealed plastic bag. Then, of course, came time. Sophie aged out of her signature look. She ceased to make history or the news. Her theory was still in textbooks, but her headshot wasn't. Out of context, her name rang bells, but more and more rarely with young people.

Liam summoned his homework onscreen.

He sheepishly introduced his problem set.

As the room quieted over the next half hour, the crowd dissolved. Daya bid Sophie goodbye and left for her next class. Meanwhile, Sophie did her best to help Liam. She gave full answers to some of his questions, but there were moments when the likeness was so arresting, she could only nod or shake her head.

"Acceleration is in meters per second *squared*?" Liam asked.

Sophie nodded.

"That's nuts."

As Liam recurved the top arch of a 2—as delicately as if it were a picture, much more than a signifier—she remembered how meticulously Jake had patted his hair into place on the morning he met her mom. She remembered Jake's neat stacks of paper, their edges aligned to sandstone smoothness. These weren't flashbacks—just memories. Hazy, precious. One by one, they confronted her with how completely she'd given her heart away and how she'd never gotten it back. She'd never been in love before or since. Time with Jake had burned her nerves beyond feeling that deeply again. She couldn't imagine ever fitting so perfectly with anyone else. The years they'd spent together felt like the most important thing she'd ever done.

"Shit," Liam said. "I got a negative speed."

Sophie blinked.

She checked Liam's math.

"Is that possible?" he asked.

"No. Speed is a scalar."

He looked stupefied.

"That means it's always positive."

"Huh."

This time, Sophie gave him clear instructions.

Liam started again.

She helped him step by step until he circled the correct number at the bottom of his tablet and closed the loop with a flourish. Sophie guided him through the rest of his problem set, explaining every concept with brilliant simplicity. She conveyed much of her advice in question form, leading him to make the inferences himself.

"We did it." Liam beamed. "Thank you."

He slid an arm through one loop of his backpack.

"The tutors don't even compare."

"Let's meet again," she said.

His smile shone on her.

They said goodbye.

Liam pushed the door open and disappeared into natural light. Sophie walked to the ladies' room, into a stall, and locked herself inside. Her hot forehead lay on the cool metal door. A son? How? For once, she was afraid of the answers.

Sophie walked home from Silliman with her spine wilting. She stopped in front of her place on Hillhouse, two doors down from where Peter and Maggie still lived. She'd refused the nineteenth-century mansion when Yale had offered it to her ten years ago—too much space just for her. Besides, she'd always lived more in her own mind than she did outside of it. The luxury would've been lost on her. But the trustees insisted that the accommodations were suitable in light of her contributions. So, she accepted the two-story, three-bedroom extravagance. She'd left the vintage furniture inside untouched. What was the difference between chairs? Sofas? Those complexities had always eluded her.

Inside, steps from the front door, she sat on a faded yellow sofa and slid her flats off to reveal toenails painted white. A navy-blue crescent moon crowned each big toe. She'd drawn them herself with a toothpick. She checked her Roxster, the same black bangle that Liam, Daya, and almost everyone else on campus wore. Ten percent of the world owned one; the device was as omnipresent as the iPhone used to be. Roxster had been Jake's largest investment at Olympus for decades and accounted for most of his double-digit returns every year. Did his investing in a watch company—in the business of time—have anything to do with her? She'd imagined an emotional pressure on his hand making the trade. Maybe he'd seen it as a way to stay close to each other without being together. But that idea always felt too narcissistic to nurture.

She revisited Jake's Personal section on Wikipedia with one hand grabbing her neck: "Kristopher is famously private. He has never carried on a relationship in the public eye. He has never been engaged or married. He has one son, Liam Carlson. His mother, Lily Carlson, is a legal aide in New York City. She and Kristopher reportedly remain on good terms."

Cold sweat chilled her.

How had she missed this? Of course, she'd read this page—dozens of times—but not in a while. She thought she'd been keeping up with him passively. He was so often on the news. She'd always checked for a wedding ring when he was on air—none. She'd googled him occasionally, but never much. The reminders that he was out there still hurt. Of course she'd read this page before, but . . . had this section been updated by then? Had she blocked it out, protecting herself? Or seen only what she wanted to see?

She typed "Lily Carlson" into the search bar, then clicked on the images filter.

Fifty different portraits appeared.

"Lily Carlson, legal aide."

One woman dominated the top row. Her professional headshot was the first hit. Sophie enlarged it. Lily had the warmest smile. Her brunette pixie cut emphasized gorgeous full cheeks. Her brown eyes beamed under thick eyebrows. Sophie imagined Lily as the kind of woman who laughed a lot, had a wide circle of friends, and said yes to every invitation.

How had she and Jake met?

How long were they together?

Did Jake like that she was upbeat? Maybe Lily was a foil to everything he struggled with himself—the isolation, the unusual devotion to one purpose—which Sophie had only magnified.

Had there been other women?

Other than Lily?

Sophie had only agreed to a handful of dates since college. After she proved block theory, some of her vibrancy returned. Maggie was so ecstatic to witness the change that, in her exuberance, she offered to set Sophie up with a neighbor's son. Sophie hadn't wanted to pop the balloon of Maggie's mood. So she'd taken Metro-North into New York City to have dinner with Hanson Lawrence, a late-thirties financier from Virginia. At the end of his first monologue, instead of asking Sophie anything, he started to detail his monthly hunting trips to Texas, where he shot big game out of a helicopter. He showed Sophie pictures of his homes in New York City, Houston, Aspen, and London. During that slideshow, Sophie stared only at his Roxster band. None of Hanson's posturing was love. It was all walls, all ego. Dinner with Hanson had preceded a few other first dates, all thanks to Maggie. Sophie never agreed to a second one.

Eventually, Maggie stopped suggesting men for Sophie. People respected her solitude as a choice. Besides, physicists were allowed more eccentricities than regular stock. Isolation was not uncommon among deep thinkers.

The sun started to set.

Windows dimmed.

In her kitchen, Sophie put on a kettle for tea. She turned its dial to summon a tight ring of blue fire. She hadn't outfitted her home with smart connectivity the way the Malchiks had. She had the same manual faucets, wood cabinets, and dumb walls as when she moved in. Whenever the Malchiks visited, they marveled at her simplicity. Her parents were the only other people she'd hosted. Isabel and Roger took the train in twice a year to attend her famous, semester-ending lectures on block theory. She visited them in return on Thanksgiving, Christmas, and the Fourth of July, at least, when she and Isabel used to hike.

It was on one of those woodsy treks years ago that they'd seen the geese near their home. Isabel had spotted them first: two elegant Canadians gliding across a glassy pond. The ground was carpeted with decaying leaves, mushroom-studded old logs, young pines, and fragrant dirt. Not a noise rippled the air. As Sophie watched them, she wondered how animals formed such strong bonds without complex language. Later that year, on the same route, she returned with Isabel to find that only one goose remained. Isabel explained that a neighbor's dog had killed the male. Geese, Isabel went on, were extremely monogamous. Not only did they mate for life, but when one was killed, the other lingered in that exact spot until forcibly removed.

The kettle screamed.

She tipped hot water into a mug.

Sophie had since then, on occasion, imagined herself as a goose still on the pond where she'd last seen Jake. Now, though, with his son.

Sophie waited for Liam in Peter's old office. She'd inherited the room and furniture when he retired. She had added a framed photo of her parents, next to one of her with the four Malchiks taken at her second New Haven Half Marathon.

Peter's wall clock ticked on.

Since Sophie met Liam last week, she'd lunched in Silliman every day. She sat in the far corner with one jelly sandwich and one iced tea. The walls intersected directly behind her—the room's spine inches behind her own—giving her the best view to watch for him. Would he dilute his blue Gatorade with ice water, the way Jake had? But she didn't want to see him just to re-see Jake. She wasn't drawn to Liam just as a nexus of information about Jake and his mother. Inexplicably, Sophie felt compelled to protect him. If this was where he ate lunch, then that's where she needed to be. But he hadn't been back yet.

Knock knock.

Liam smiled in her doorway.

"Hi!" She rose to shake his hand.

He wore a light pink linen shirt. Its wrinkles gave the fabric depth and left the nuances of his chest a mystery. Sophie gestured for him to join her at the round table and felt Professor

Malchik's stiff arm in her own. He'd offered her a seat just like this the first time they'd met. Liam sat with his tablet in front of him. Sophie barely looked at it. Up close, now, she saw the Lily in him. Her cheekbones had been stunning, distinct as a heart on each side of her smile. Those widened Liam's face more than Jake's. Lily's small, effeminate mouth softened his jaw. Sophie saw other parts of Lily, too, not in perfect replicas but in traces.

She forced herself to speak.

"How are you?" she asked.

"Good!" He gave a thumbs-up.

White paint speckled his hand.

"Did you paint this morning?"

He looked at his hand and laughed.

"How can you tell?" he asked. He scratched his head. Freckles dusted the rim of his ear. A lone brown one dotted behind his lobe. She wouldn't have expected much sun to shine there.

"What're you working on?"

"My graduation show. It's still a couple months away, but it's supposed to be my best work since I've been here. It's always harder when you care."

"True."

Pause.

Liam tapped his tablet until his problem set appeared.

"So—" he began.

"Do you like it here?" she asked.

She interlaced veiny hands on the table. Her narrow shoulders faced him.

"I do," he admitted.

She waited.

"The people, most of all," he went on. "I met Daya here. And it's a beautiful school. I get to do what I love." He smiled to punctuate the happy thought.

"What do you want to do after graduating?"

"Paint. I'd like to do that every day, as much as I can."

She waited.

"Which means I'll have to sell more of my work. Or my work for more." He laughed. "Thankfully, there'll be a few dealers at the show. I've been told they help get you into galleries and whatnot." He yielded again to the curiosity evident in her silence. "But it's less that I want to *get* anywhere. It's more that I care about what I'm doing day to day."

"Interesting."

"Thanks."

"Have you been getting the help you need in the art department?"

She squinted, serious.

"They're fantastic." Had anyone else asked him that before? Aside from Daya, maybe? He sat up straighter. "Mostly because they trust me. My advisor and I agree art should reflect what's inside you. Great art is a blend of your experiences, the time.

"Daya and I went to a Dada exhibit last week. It wasn't my taste. The collages were abrasive, violent. They mashed up industrial elements, body parts, and magazine cutouts like ransom letters. But that's a reflection of the era. That's why it was great art. I think artists as a category are people drawn to express the world around them. Within that, different artists choose different tools. For some, it's painting, or sculpture, collages, or—"

"Physics?"

She smiled.

"For you, maybe. Not me."

"Are you on track for your show?"

"Yes. Barring one last painting, but I'll finish that eventually."

She waited.

And waited.

He smiled.

"All right," she said at last. "Shall we?"

Liam sat dumbfounded on a sunny bench, having just left Sophie's office.

Who *was* she?

She'd been too generous for him still to know so little about her. After taking a tender, unhurried interest in his art, she'd guided him through simple math for an hour. She never lost her patience. She dignified every one of his dense questions with her full attention. She didn't even answer her phone when it rang. She acted as if there was nowhere else she'd rather be than reviewing basic physics. After they solved the final problem, she offered to help him again next week. Of course, he'd agreed. But weren't teaching assistants and tutors invented to protect faculty time? He felt bad imposing on this middle-aged woman.

He raised his Roxster wrist and searched "Sophie, Yale physics" using the images filter. One *million* results? Were there really a million photos of her? Or related to her? He scrolled down. President Cohan? A much younger Sophie shook his hand by the unmistakable columns of the White House. In the next thumbnail, Sophie stood next to the Obamas in black tie at a Nobel Prize award ceremony. She'd won in physics. Then, Sophie was pictured walking by the Brazilian embassy in Buenos Aires. The embassy was a domed building like the US Congress. The caption mentioned a global scientific conference where Sophie was the keynote speaker. Liam enlarged the next image: Sophie Jones, the Halloween costume.

Wow.

Sophie Jones.

Of course.

From block theory.

He'd learned about that in high school. Sophie had proved it with the Malchik theorem. Everyone who'd lived through that moment said its memory endured in tragedy-level detail. The event had touched people around the world. Isaac Newton, Albert Einstein, and Stephen Hawking, scientific names engraved on everyone's consciousness—even painters'—Sophie *Jones* was among them. The woman he'd just taken for granted wasn't *a* Sophie, but *the* Sophie. She stood behind the insight of the century.

So why did she care about him? On his way out the door, she'd asked how he was finding the dining halls. Did he like the food Yale served? Was he staying hydrated? It was like a conversation with his mother—if she were gifted with concentration.

Lily was a free spirit: loving and nonjudgmental, but not the most attentive parent. She'd never been able to pin down a specific time to meet. Instead, she suggested a half-hour range, and she was rarely on time for that. She served dinner at a different time every night. Sometimes, while he was at Trinity, they would eat at 6 p.m. in their apartment on Ninetieth and Lexington. Sometimes they ate at 9 p.m. There was never any way of telling in advance which end of the spectrum they'd be on that evening. Of course she asked Liam questions about himself, but never such specific ones and never so many in a row. Her approach to life was visceral—which was perfectly all right. At the end of the day, he was happy. Healthy. At Yale.

But Sophie had really listened.

Sophie *Jones*.

He covered his eyes, embarrassed. His physics class was a survey designed for non-science majors. He knew his homework was cringingly simple even as he struggled to grasp it. Wasn't she supposed to be preoccupied with grander thoughts about space and time? Much more than his student art show? People in her stratum were supposed to be busy. His dad was. Liam barely knew him. Besides, weren't geniuses smug? Didn't they take advantage of being idolized? Picasso had been famously nightmarish in person. Of the seven major women in his life, two had gone insane and two had committed suicide. Sophie had been kind. Why didn't the world's most brilliant woman have any idea of her own importance?

*   *   *

Liam showed up next week in a pristine white oxford and belted khakis. He stepped into Sophie's office looking like a senatorial version of himself.

"Good afternoon," he greeted.

They shook hands.

"How are you?" she asked kindly.

"I'm doing well."

"How's your art show coming?"

They filled their old seats.

"Coming along." Sophie sensed something left unsaid. "Did some sketching today. And more work on these problems than I'm used to. I really tried my best."

This time, when Liam opened his homework on the tablet, the space under each problem showed tattered equations instead of the typical, unattempted white. He seemed more anxious than usual. Had he googled her? Told his parents about her? Afternoon sun warmed the room. As Liam pushed his sleeves up to his elbows, Sophie's eyes were drawn uncontrollably to the familiar dark hair on his forearms. His seashell bracelet cozied up to his Roxster. It was like seeing a picture of somewhere she used to live, now different, but still home.

Liam pulled a palm-size sketchbook out of his back pocket. He rested it off to the side on the table, drawing Sophie's eyes.

"What were you sketching?" she asked.

"My last piece for the show."

She waited.

"I start everything in pencil." He peeled the cover back to the first page. Daya's face was drawn in moonlight gray. The likeness was startling, except he'd replaced her hair with flower stems that blossomed below her collarbone. "This is a portrait that'll be on display."

"It's beautiful."

"Thank you."

"Is there a theme to your show?"

"Not intentionally," he admitted. "But every piece does connect back to one of my relationships." He flipped to a second sketch of Daya. This one replaced her body with a curving flower stem. Leaves sprouted up her arms. It reminded Sophie of a Salvador Dalí painting, *The Burning Giraffe*. In it, the central figure had cabinet drawers stacked up one of her legs. Another drawer replaced her bust. She stood in the desert while a distant giraffe burned red down its spine—in a shockingly imaginative way. Sophie loved Dalí. Liam had the same impulse to braid fantasy into reality, but in his hands, the braid came out beautiful.

He dragged his thumb down the rest of the booklet, playing a slideshow of sketches. His finger pinned the final one to cardboard. That narrow profile—but transformed. Jake's mouth was a clockface. His suit jacket was covered in the word ROXSTER. Liam had apparently rejected the image by scratching zigzags on top. Black, destructive thunderbolts struck some of the details. Liam closed the book.

He forced a laugh.

"Still working on that one," he said.

The portrait was so unflattering that Sophie felt compelled to stick up for Jake.

"He's a complex man."

Liam froze.

Of course Sophie knew Jake. She'd admitted that when they met. Her comment about their resemblance had led Liam to believe she'd known Jake in college. Another professor had introduced himself in a similar random encounter on Cross Campus. That man, Dr. Richards, had taken Cold War with Jake and now taught history here. Whatever connection Sophie'd had to Jake, Liam had assumed it was superficial, brief. Jake didn't nurture relationships with anyone, not even with Lily and him, Jake's own family. But Sophie's comment—*"He's a complex man"*—was too loving. It showed more familiarity than Liam had expected. Suddenly, he understood why she helping him: she'd actually been close to Jake.

"Hm. Well . . . you probably know him better than I do." He shrugged, vulnerable. "My biological father and I don't really talk."

"I'm sorry."

"Don't be. That's life."

His tone sagged. As he drew inward, Sophie's pity came out. She'd struggled with the same fate: a permanent connection to Jake. She wanted to make sure Liam was okay.

She pointed at the sketchbook.

"What did you want that picture to say?" she asked.

Sophie looked so genuinely concerned that he wanted to tell her more. Besides, he'd always been an open person, and he liked talking to her. She was an exceptional listener, as if she had four ears and two hearts.

"You really want to know?" he asked.

She nodded.

"Well, like I said, great art shows what's inside of you. So, the answer to your question is a little personal—if you're okay with that."

She nodded again.

He inhaled.

"I don't know how much of this you know already. My mom and Jake weren't together long before I showed up. A few months. I don't think he wanted Mom to have me. To go through with it, I mean. She's never said that, and I doubt he ever said that explicitly, but . . . He's a good person. He's always paid my tuition, but I never spent weekends with him. You see what I mean? He just wasn't around. He was a provider, but I don't think he ever wanted to be my dad." Liam winced as if the word tasted bad. "Mom says he's 'cold,' but . . ."

He shook his head.

"But . . ." Sophie prompted.

"It isn't that he's indifferent. He cares a lot—but about his work. He really does think he's fulfilling his destiny by going to work every day. Most people think about what they do as just a job, but *his* job has to be, like, an expression of his soul." Liam paused. "I get that a little bit, because I paint, but it's not the same. He doesn't seem to enjoy things. My theory is, I think he got hurt, and he went like a clam." He shut his hands like shells hinged at the wrist. "He shut himself off from the world, maybe. I don't know."

"I'm sorry."

"For what?"

She lowered her head.

"Bringing him up," she said.

"It's okay."

He smiled to reassure her.

"I email him every few months to tell him how I'm doing. Sometimes he responds." He shrugged. "But my mom has always been there."

His tablet went to screensaver.

"So you knew Jake in college?" he asked.

"Yes."

"What was he like?"

Sophie remembered lying next to Jake on Berkeley's hammock their sophomore year. The setting sun lit a yellow edge over the college around them. A paperback of *Star Dust: Poems* lay tented on her chest, just like *New Haven: Reshaping the City, 1900–1980* did on Jake's. He was supposed to be reading chapter three for one of his classes. His green polo was tattered around the sleeves and collar. Sophie eyed his tan skin through the holes.

"Who would I eat with?" he asked.

"Yes," Sophie confirmed her question. "If you could have dinner tonight with anyone, me excluded, who would it be?"

"Probably my dad."

They rocked back and forth.

"Why?" she asked.

"Just to see how he's doing. What he's like."

Liam's question remained.

"What was he like?"

She united the two tips of her shirt collar.

"He was driven. A hard worker. Intense. I'm sure you know all of that." She tried to say enough without giving away too much. She didn't want to admit to her relationship with Jake, which might make Liam uneasy and drive him away. "But I never thought he was selfish. Some people want to achieve for their ego, but I always thought he was motivated by other people. He was in it for something bigger than himself."

Liam nodded.

"A lot of people here are like that," he said. "Driven, I mean. They hunker down and shut others out, but Jake takes it to an extreme. I *care* about my work, of course, but I care more about Daya. My mom. The ones around me." He paused. "When you're balanced, people look down on you. You get judged when you care about relationships as much as work. Nobody says that, but you can tell. It's not something that people here really respect."

"That sounds familiar."

Liam waited.

"Something similar happened to me," Sophie went on delicately. "In undergrad, I started to care more about my relationships—

well, one in particular—and people thought I wasn't reaching my potential. I never liked how that was framed, as if it's a trade-off between love and work. Love enhances everything." She breathed deeply. "That might sound strange, coming from me. I know how I'm seen. I'll be remembered for my theorem, for my mind. People don't see that my greatest gift was really . . ." *My heart.* "Anyway, I don't have a stake in how I'm remembered, but it's interesting to me that it's so misleading."

She lowered her gaze, saw the tablet.

"Well," she went on. "We should probably do some physics."

Liam returned to Sophie's office again one week later.

And again.

And again.

Every Thursday at 4 p.m., they assumed the same seats at her round table. At least half of their conversations had nothing to do with physics. Sophie dug him up question by question. Where did he grow up? With his mom on the Upper East Side. Where did he consider home? Wherever Daya was. How long had they been together? They met during freshman assembly. She was wearing a bright orange dress and golden hoop earrings that, whenever she laughed, dazzled like glinting equators. Had he always wanted to paint? Yes. Growing up, he drew compulsively on the walls of his mom's apartment: skinny crescent moons, stars in dense packs, and the sun in a perfect circle. Why did he focus on images of outer space? He only saw Jake a couple times a year, when Jake arrived carrying a magazine covered in stars.

"Thank you for your time," Liam said.

They ended every Thursday that way.

Meanwhile, Liam bought a new sketchbook from the Yale Bookstore. He needed to finish his portrait of Jake. The rest of his show was complete: three canvases of Daya, two of Lily, and two of Berkeley, his dorm of four years, painted first as a freshman and then in diptych as a senior. Page after page, Liam sketched versions of Jake, but nothing felt honest enough. He crossed every image out with lightning slashes. Sophie had asked if he had a good relationship with Jake, and to be honest, Liam wasn't sure. Maybe the other portraits had been easier to finish because he knew how the subjects made him feel.

"Is that it?" Liam asked.

He tapped the number he'd just written on his tablet and squinted his eyes into doubtful slits. Sophie read the math from top to bottom and then paused.

He'd been here an hour, and they'd only just started his problem set. Was he sleeping all right? How was Daya? The amount of time Sophie spent looking after him—on top of the enormous privilege of her private tutoring—was starting to feel wrong. He rubbed his eyes. She was too kind. He'd tried to balance the conversational scale between them, but her modesty made that almost impossible. Wikipedia had filled in some of the gaps, so he knew she'd never married or had any children. He knew she lived on Hillhouse and was famously introverted, but the rest of her personal life was a black box. How exactly had she known Jake in college? He never did ask. The question felt intrusive.

"Why'd you become a professor?" he asked.

"Hm?" Sophie asked.

He stopped rubbing his eyes.

"Is it out?" Jake asked in their double. His left eye welled with tears and surface tension. He blinked. A thin river ran down his face. Sophie studied him with her hands on his shoulders still drenched from his run outside.

"Yes," she declared. "Bug no more."

"Are my eyes okay?" he asked.

Her expression was stern.

"Soph, what color are my eyes?"

"They're white. You've been cursed."

"Soph! I'm serious."

"I'm sorry. You're fine, honest."

"The thing flew right into my eye."

Jake looked nervous.

"I promise," she said. "I looked."

"Okay. Thank you."

"It's just a little bit of a curse."

"Sophie!" He grinned.

"Really small."

He laughed.

"All right, all right," he said. "You know, you're lucky I love you."

She kissed his forehead.

"Yes," she said. "I am."

"I just feel like I'm wasting your time," Liam admitted. "I really appreciate it. I feel very lucky, but . . . I don't know. Did you want to teach?"

Liam's pink eyelids stuck to his own teary dew. Sophie gazed at him with affection. He looked tortured by the prospect of imposing on her. She decided she couldn't dodge all of his questions. She mirrored his lean against the back of her chair.

"Well, I didn't really mean to end up here."

"Huh," Liam said. "You come across as a planner."

She smiled.

"You really want to know?" she asked.

"Yes."

Sophie tilted her head to the side.

"For me, it was about understanding things I couldn't see," she explained.

"What do you mean?"

"Oh, it's boring."

She tucked hair behind her ear.

"It's not boring at all," he insisted.

"Okay," she said tentatively. "Well, take air." She gestured around them. "It's here, and it's invisible to us, but really, it's nitrogen, oxygen, carbon dioxide, and argon. It clings to our planet because of gravity; it moves around us in whirls we feel as wind and weather; and it carries sound waves." Liam didn't seem to follow. "Or take magnetic force. Earth has its own magnetic field, and it runs from deep underground into space. That field protects us from harmful particles shed by the sun." Liam still looked stumped. "Or take streamers. The electricity in the air before lightning strikes? My point is that you can't see any of these things, but you can feel them, and physics can prove them to you. You can't see them, but physics shows you they're there."

"Huuuuh." He stretched the syllable.

"Does that make sense?"

He nodded.

"Things you can't see, but you know they're there."

"Yes," she said.

"Like some people."

"Exactly."

A knock on the door shook them both.

"Professor Jones?" A mousy girl stuck her head inside.

Liam stood.

"Thank you," he said hurriedly.

He picked up his tablet—nearly blank.

"We didn't finish," Sophie protested.

"You've been extremely helpful. And I do have a painting to . . ." He waved an invisible paintbrush. "Thank you for your time."

"It's all the same."

*　　*　　*

Sophie stepped up to the podium for her last lecture of the semester. Today, she'd explain her famous proof, the Malchik theorem. The auditorium was packed, buzzing with conversation. People crammed into the aisle between rows and sat cross-legged on the carpet. More and more people kept trickling in now dangerously close to the 2 p.m. start.

Peter sat in the front row next to Maggie. They'd arrived twenty minutes early as they always did for this lecture. His cheeks were plumper than the sharp edges they used to be. His jawbones no longer converged into an arrowhead chin. Sandy brown age spots freckled his happy face. Everything about him was softer, which Maggie attributed to "peace of mind." On Maggie's other side, Isabel and Ronald sat holding hands next to their caretaker, a young nurse named Jolene. Isabel's nails were painted white as her hair. Sophie smiled.

"Good morning," she said.

Even with a gentle voice, she commanded attention.

"Today, I'll describe the Malchik theorem . . ."

Peter remembered when he'd first read that name on their train ride into Cambridge. Sophie had been about to scribe her proof before a stadium-size audience of their most sophisticated peers. News crews were already on-site waiting to break the story of her success or failure. The last page of her proof lay on Peter's lap. He'd been going through the hundred pages of her journal line by line before Sophie presented that afternoon just in case she forgot something and needed him to feed her the next step. She hadn't asked for this, but he'd wanted to help. Peter had just come across the three-word title at the very end: "The Malchik Theorem."

> *"Thank you," Peter said sincerely.*
> *English countryside rolled by their window.*
> *Sophie removed an earbud.*
> *Did he hear Ray Charles?*
> *"Thank you," Peter repeated.*
> *"Of course."*

Sophie never explained why she hadn't named it after herself. Peter had assumed that part of it was she wanted as little attention as possible. Part of it, though, must have been affection for him and Maggie—that she did value the time he'd devoted to her since her freshman year, that she did feel part of the home they'd opened to her leading up to that pivotal day.

> *After her presentation, Peter and Sophie hunched over two baskets of fish and chips in the back of a dark pub in England. Peter only ate a couple of French fries. He stared at the red checkered tablecloth while Sophie downed her grape soda and kept eating long after he'd finished. Peter wrung his hands, struggling to find the right words.*
> *What Peter was trying to articulate was: he knew Sophie was driven by loss. When she stayed late in his living room*

to ask more questions, she wasn't just looking for insight. She was looking for him, whoever he was, or for whatever it was that they'd had. But as Peter sat in that pub with Sophie—knowing the thousands of hours it had taken her to get there, the commitment through setbacks, the persistence through plateaus, and the mind-boggling number of normal life experiences she'd forfeited for the sake of this uncertain endeavor—it dawned on him that Sophie had proven something else. Maybe it was something only he could see. There was the math on the whiteboard, and that was one thing. But he saw another proof in Sophie's life. Through her choices, she'd proven beyond a shadow of a doubt her own love for the one she'd lost. Peter wanted to tell Sophie how much he admired not just her mind, but her heart, and he was as proud as if . . . But none of the words seemed to fit.

Peter glanced sideways at Maggie. He reached for her hand and squeezed it, as proud as if Sophie were one of their own.

Minutes into class, the back door opened and clicked shut. Three more Yalies trickled in and disappeared into the crowd behind the last row. Sophie lost her train of thought. How many eyes were in this room? At least four hundred studied her. She shrunk her world down to familiar faces: her parents, the Malchiks, the woman who'd raised her hand every few slides all semester to ask a question, the man who'd eaten an entire bowl of cereal every lecture, and his friend who'd always used the chair in front of him as a footrest.

Liam and Daya entered through the back door. They held hands as they crept hunchbacked down the center aisle and across the front row to sit on the floor ten feet from the podium. Liam waved at Sophie until Daya forced his arm down.

Sophie smiled.

"As I was saying . . ."

Students lined up for Sophie after class. Her parents avoided the uproar by leaving with Jolene and the Malchiks. Sophie greeted everyone who waited their turn. At the end of the line, Liam stood with an arm around Daya. Between handshakes, Sophie checked on them in the back. Daya wore denim overalls cut off above the knee. Liam's tee had a foot-long, apostrophic slash of silver paint on one side. Liam never looked more like Jake than when he was kissing Daya's temple or squeezing her arm. The young couple didn't seem to notice the irksome wait at all. Sophie shook hand after hand until it was only the three of them left.

"Sophie!" Liam hugged her. "That blew my mind."

"Thank you for coming."

"Well, we weren't just here for the physics." Liam fished a catalog from his pocket. On the cover, a painted lightning bolt struck earth. Comets ricocheted out of the point of collision.

The impossible scene was strangely beautiful. The next page read, "Intertwined: Liam Carlson's Graduation Art Show." The subtitle "Thanks to" presided over a long list of names. Liam pointed to the middle of the stack, "Dr. Sophie Jones."

"We'd be honored if you'd come," he said.

Daya nodded.

"Not just because you helped me pass physics." Liam laughed. "Our talks inspired one of my pieces. I'd love to tell you more about it at the show."

Sophie studied the catalog as she climbed Hillhouse. Her head felt bloodless, brainless. She texted her parents and the Malchiks on the same thread to say she wasn't feeling well, that she thought she should be alone tonight. She'd see them soon at graduation next week.

Would he be there?

Sophie shut the door to her house behind her. She dropped her keys on the silver console in the front hall.

Of course he'd be there.

Wouldn't he?

Sophie climbed narrow stairs to the first floor and then a second flight to the attic. The roof sloped. Crouching, she moved a plastic bin of winter boots aside to reveal a shoebox covered in dust. She carried it downstairs to the living room sofa. Inside the box, a mound of envelopes were addressed to her. The delicate papers were tinged off-white. She removed faded loose-leaf inside one and unfolded a letter thin as tissue. His blue pen print read:

Sophie,

Merry Christmas! By the time you read this, you'll be home, I'll be at my place, and we won't have seen each other for a few days. In case you aren't feeling it right now, over there where I can't hold you: I am out-of-this-world in love with you.

As I think about what was going on in my life last year, I never imagined that someone—you—would come into my life and sweep me off my feet. These months together have been a dream. I can't say it enough: you're beautiful, fascinating, kind, and you amaze me every day. You listen whenever I say anything, and you hear what I mean. It's easy to be romantic on special occasions. But when I see your face after I come back from the gym, or when I meet you on Science Hill, my heart jumps like nothing I've felt before. Every day, I wake up astonished at how we got here and, frankly, that this exists. I feel incredibly lucky to have found this one other person who understands me. I've never met anyone before who just understands.

Even when I'm not there—all of that is true.

See you soon.

Love,

Jake

Sophie put the letter next to her on the sofa.

She unwrapped another.

Sophie,

Time flies when you're having fun. It seems like just yesterday we were sitting next to each other for the first time in psych. In case I haven't told you any of this recently, for your twentieth (!) birthday (!), I say it again. Sophie, I love it when:

- *You hold my leg when we're sitting side by side.*
- *You slow the kiss down and run your hands through my hair.*
- *You tilt your head to the side when you're thinking hard about something.*
- *You teach me before we go to sleep.*
- *You leave me notes around our room.*
- *You answer "I love you" with "I know."*
- *You make me feel like I can accomplish anything.*
- *You make me want to be better without making me feel like I need to change. I've always had big dreams, but being with you gives them meaning.*

For this and much more, I want you to know that, to me, you are perfect. Every day, I feel so lucky to have met you. I hope you had a great birthday, and I can't wait to spend many, many more with you.

I love you with all my heart.

Jake

She read letter after letter, avoiding a particular envelope until it was the only one left. The *Sophie* on it was slanted, hurried.

Jake had given her this on the day he postponed his birthday dinner with her senior year. He'd forgotten all about their plans until after Sophie had started cooking for them. It was the last letter he'd written her.

> *Sophie,*
>
> *I'm so sorry for losing track of time.*
>
> *I want to take this moment to say something I can't say enough: my love, you are rare and extraordinary. I know you hate to be singled out, but it's important to me that you know how special you are. Even if you won't admit it.*
>
> *I realize things are not the way they should be right now, but I also know that nothing is stronger than our love for each other. Things are messy and tough, but life is messy and tough. In the end, this will only make us better and stronger.*
>
> *Love,*
>
> *Jake*

Sophie rested the note on her gut.

CHAPTER 13

Jake stopped in his lap pool and panted before the transformed New York City skyline. Goggles clung to his hairline above deep wrinkles as he gazed at the green panorama. Since college, warmer temperatures had brought the ocean into Manhattan, filling new canals, marshes, and grassy spaces. He checked the stalled timer on his Roxster: forty-five minutes. He stepped out of the pool and dried himself on the way to his master bathroom.

Walking through the empty apartment, he passed bare wall after bare wall. His decorator had propped enormous photographs—a portrait of Muhammad Ali, photos of horses caught mid-gallop—against the walls in dozens of places. Jake had promised to hang them, but the truth was that the blankness felt right. He still had more to do. This wasn't where he was supposed to stop. He hadn't furnished the place aside from his bedroom and a sofa in the living room, so his penthouse retained an uninhabited quality. He had no guests.

As Jake showered, headlines scrolled across the glass next to a display of his physical stats. He scanned them while washing his hair. When the water stopped, the news disappeared, and Jackie Wilson's classic, soulful voice filled the apartment. Technology had leapt ahead, but Jake still loved that song "(Your Love Keeps Lifting Me) Higher & Higher." He knew it by heart—a gorgeous internal tattoo.

His walk-in closet contained a long horseshoe of suit jackets hanging over a ring of pants. Shelves flanked him, filled with over one hundred pairs of similar loafers and sneakers. He dressed in a gray tee and lightweight suit jacket. Every day, a different version of the same outfit. He stuck to metallic shades in the same color palette as armor. In the elevator down to the lobby, he checked his neat reflection. He'd had the same haircut for most of his life.

He hopped in the back of a black car.

"Boss," the car's masculine AI greeted.

"Carl, please route to Olympus."

Jake sat on a honey-colored seat. He read the news on his watch until they reached his office building in midtown.

"Boss, we have arrived."

Jake kept reading.

"Boss, we have arrived."

The alert repeated at higher and higher volumes.

"Carl, stop. Carl, what's the weather today?"

"Today, expect a high of eighty-two degrees and a low of seventy-three degrees with clear skies."

Outside, the dense air felt tropical. One Madison Avenue welcomed Jake back with air-conditioning. As he rose in the elevator up to Olympus, he scrolled through new emails—From: Carlson, Liam. No message preview. When Jake tapped to open it, a lightning bolt dominated his screen. He swiped to the next page which announced "Intertwined" as the title of Liam's art show followed by a list of acknowledgments—*Dr. Sophie Jones.*

The elevator doors opened.

Jake stood still.

The doors started to shut.

His arm flew forward.

How did they know each other?

He stepped forward into Olympus, which filled the top floor. Above him, thick white beams sloped up, down, and sideways like roller-coaster tracks. The rafters were packed with plants: ferns, spear-leaved snake plants, dark green ivy with leaves down every tendril, and spider plants with long white arms. Jake walked down the central path dividing the office in half. Most of the analysts stood as they worked on clear touch screens at eye level. These hovered by magnetic suspension, barely distinguishable from the air around them. Only in passing did their round edges glimmer.

Jake shut the door to his office behind him.

He sat down.

His stomach shrunk.

Would she be at Liam's show?

*   *   *

Right after Sophie had proved block theory, Jake had gone to sleep every night with the same fantasy vignette in mind: meeting again in New Haven. He imagined she'd reply to his email with thoughtful lines of her own. They'd schedule a time to find each other again in Blue State or Ashley's, or on Cross Campus. During the day, between distracted meetings, he researched online to prepare for that moment. He searched for any science on "first love reunions." Google would prompt in the "People Also Ask" sidebar:

What is first love?

Why is first love so special?

Why is the first love hardest to forget?

But most articles Jake found on "first love reunions" were fluff pieces in ten-point lists or slideshows where half the slides were ads. He stayed in that place of scattered reading for a week, not getting any half-decent information, but hopeful he'd find some, until the day she mentioned, "I have some ideas."

Then, he let the fantasy go.

A few months later, he met Dr. Chuck Bradley at a fundraiser hosted by Olympus in New York City. The Midtown Cipriani's high, painted ceilings paled in comparison to the black-tie crowd on its floor. All proceeds went to Empower Now, a charity devoted to breaking the cycle of poverty. Jake was already making waves as a philanthropist. He sat on Empower Now's board; he personally funded education initiatives in bad neighborhoods; he visited high schools in the city to expose kids to finance; and he skimmed every résumé sent to Olympus that had been rejected for inexperience.

On that particular night, while in line for the bar, Chuck introduced himself as a social scientist at New York University.

Jake shook his hand.

"What are you working on?" Jake asked.

"First love," Chuck said.

Chuck said he was doing survey work on people who'd met their first love much later in life. Jake proceeded to ask a string of questions so passionately and precisely worded that he worried Chuck might wrongly perceive him as a potential benefactor. Chuck scribbled a list of relevant journal articles on a cocktail napkin.

"But those are just background," Chuck said.

"What do you mean?" Jake asked.

Chuck said his new article, "Love Interrupted," was the missing link in the literature. No one had looked at first love over a long enough time period. So, ten years prior, Chuck had identified 1,002 American couples in their late teens or early twenties who'd been dating for at least a year and claimed to be in love for the first time. Last year, he had contacted all of them. Twenty-three had been separated by circumstances—moving for a job or for school, most commonly—*and* had definite plans to meet up with their love again. Chuck interviewed them before and after the reunion. The results would be published in a peer-reviewed journal in two months.

Chuck then went on a tangent about how rare great research in psychology was becoming as it faced underfunding. "Dry period," Chuck repeated. His palm stayed open as he bemoaned the challenges. Jake only nodded.

"Love Interrupted" came out on schedule.

Jake read it immediately.

Chuck had found that ten years later, 73 percent of the initial 2,004 people thought their first love was the greatest romance of their lives. Chuck had asked people to rank its specific traits as compared to those of relationships since. In this survey, the majority said their first love was the most trusting, vulnerable, sexual, dependent, euphoric, and painful romance of their lives. Across the board, first love was the most intense on every metric. Chuck explained this by saying that the best predictor of relationship caliber was the amount of quality time spent together. He referenced a shelf's worth of research for support—some of which he'd recommended to Jake—and then summarized at the end, "The key to love is time." When people were young, they were rich with it. They could funnel it in massive volumes into a relationship. "The chance to grow a relationship that deep almost never happens again."

Jake had only read the first ten dense pages of Chuck's article when he realized Tawny was standing in his office, reminding him of a meeting starting then. His five-person team assembled monthly to present new investment ideas. In the boardroom, his colleagues' slideshows were lost on him as he mulled *the key to love is time.*

An hour later, Jake resumed reading. Another predictor of relationship quality was a couple's personal beliefs about love. Young people idealized romance. They believed true love was real, spectacular, and lasted forever, so they saw it in their relationships. To support this, Chuck cited research on how expectations influenced perception. As people aged, it became harder to keep a rose-tinted view of life. People lived long enough to see friends or family disappoint them, dreams falter, disease strike, or other misfortunes. It took a rare character to stay idealistic and re-create the first love experience they had back when they saw the best in people. Chuck wrote, "To find true love, you have to believe in it."

At last, Jake reached the section "Survey Results of 23 First-Love Reunions One Decade Later." By then, it had been almost that long since he'd last seen her. He inhaled. Apparently, obsessive thinking about the reunion usually consumed couples as soon as the plan was made. Right after Sophie proved block theory, he had succumbed to that. Jake didn't scroll on. Instead, he remembered Chuck's open palm as they stood in the ballroom. Jake suddenly didn't like the fact that the man behind this research had so quickly segued into a discussion about money. Who was this Chuck Bradley anyway? What made him the expert on love?

Jake never finished the article. It had been nearly twenty-five years since he started it, and he still didn't know the outcome of the couples' meetings. The truth was that he didn't want those reunions to end badly. If they'd failed, he didn't want to know about them. He needed to believe that if he met Sophie again . . .

When was Liam's show?

May 18, 2048.

Liam had invited Jake to art shows before. Jake had never gone, but he pored over the catalog every time. He learned something when he looked at Liam's work. Each piece re-arranged the world so completely that it woke Jake up to how much more was possible. Two years ago, Liam had painted Lily under a strange new tree: the leaves were enormous apple slices. Each cross-section was heart-shaped, red skins looping around white middles. The tree grew out of a colossal apple that sat unplanted on grassy ground. Lily leaned against the trunk. *My Mom the Miracle Tree* captured her beautiful nonsense.

Janice had visited two of Liam's shows and had apparently met his longtime girlfriend, Daya. Janice's hallmark quality was still her reliability. At seventy-five, she was living out her retirement in a Park Avenue apartment that Jake had bought for her on the Upper East Side. She'd already booked her trip into New Haven for Liam's graduation day.

Jake checked his May calendar.

Jake waited for Lily in Gotta Robota, a grab-and-go restaurant by his office without human employees. The air-conditioning was crisp. Jake interlaced his fingers on the picnic-style table. The time of 11:55 a.m. glowed lightsaber blue on his watch.

Last week, right after Liam had emailed his invite, Lily had forwarded Jake that same message and asked if he was going to the show. Jake didn't respond. He and Lily were on good terms, all things considered. He just wasn't sure yet. He doubted this was the right way to see Sophie again. She was acutely sensitive. Every detail mattered. With Liam and Lily there . . . This reunion would be a far cry from the fantasies he used to carry with him. Jake's lack of response had led to a request to meet in person.

11:57 a.m.

Jake still didn't know what to tell Lily. He'd woken up every day this week in a sweat. His body had never rebelled like this before. His whole life, his limbs had bowed to discipline. He'd never been seriously ill. Now, sweat soaked his gray sheets every morning, turning them black in cloudlike splotches strewn with blurry handprints. He kept dreaming he was on trial. The blurry prosecutor was charging Jake with "absence in the first degree."

12:00 p.m.

Touch-screen menus lined the walls below eye level. Each person input their order on one of the screens. Then, the menu lifted like a drawbridge to reveal their meal. Most people in Gotta Robota carried their white bowls of food out the door. Those who stayed ate alone. Jake checked his wrist and gritted his teeth. It annoyed him that no one outside of finance seemed to understand the value of time—well, almost no one.

12:05 p.m.

12:15 p.m.

He'd said noon, but Lily had always been on another wavelength. They'd met at a bake sale hosted by Olympus. That afternoon, the sky had been baby blue. Olympus was offering brownies on Twenty-Sixth and Park Avenue South in exchange for a donation to Empower Now. Jake was sitting next to Tawny at a folding table. Lily stopped in front of him wearing white flats scuffed gray, jean shorts unraveling at the hem, and a crop top he recognized from an H&M ad. Her whole outfit cost $15, but she reached for her phone instantly and Venmo'd their team $5. Jake found her generosity attractive. She'd only invited him to her place a few times in six months when she asked him to sit down for a conversation in her living room. She told him that she was pregnant and she'd always wanted to be a mom.

Life had gotten so out of control.

What was that called again?

"Entropy is the scientific word for chaos." Sophie's voice was soft. Jake curled around her, his head on the natural pillow under her ribs. "In our universe, entropy is always increasing. This room, bed, us—everything gets more disordered over time." Jake kissed her belly button. He scooched down to kiss the waistband of his boxers around her hips.

"Things with you get better, though."

"I know." She rubbed his head. *"It's not saying things get better or worse, just messier. Our clothes will fall apart. We'll get old. The things we own will break. Entropy."*

"Jake!" Lily smiled.

12:21 p.m.

He stood.

Lily spread her tanned arms. Her sundress looked like an elongated T-shirt. The hem at her knees danced with every step. Her brown flip-flops reminded him that there wasn't a dress code at Howards & Levine, the law office where she worked defending tenants facing eviction. She hugged Jake and pressed two hands—no rings—onto his back.

"Hi, Lily."

Jake gestured for her to sit. When she did, her legs crossed easily and her white smile spread wide. He remembered there was no misery to Lily. Her feelings could get hurt, and she could get emotional about Liam, but she had no deep-rooted suffering. She had a drifting, happy quality that had never meshed with his own sense of purpose. She slept in. She forgot to pay some of her bills. She forgot to take her birth control every day—Jake should have paid more attention to that confession. Jake had a soft spot for young hearts, but Lily's mind was young, too. He figured it was part of why they'd never quite clicked.

"How are you?" Lily asked.

"Great, how are you?"

His standard reply was monotone.

Silence answered. Meanwhile, he wondered if he and Sophie started talking to each other again, would they ever stop? If he went to the art show—

"Jake?" Lily asked.

"Great, how are you?" he asked.

Lily nodded.

"It really is good to see you," she said. "I know how busy you are, so the fact that you're here . . . It's really nice to be on the same side." Jake imagined sitting next to Sophie in the dining hall. "You know, on the same parenting team? For Liam."

"What?"

"The same team. For Liam."

"Right."

"I didn't want Liam's invite to get lost. I know you have so much to do." She clasped her hands as if she were praying. "I'm here to ask in person if you can come to his show and graduation? It's so important to Liam you're there. It means so much to him."

Jake fanned himself with the crew neck of his tee.

"Jake?" she prompted.

"Hm?"

"Liam's graduation. His—"

Four years ago, Carl parked on a street full of teens milling in dark gowns and caps, yellow tassels orbiting happy faces. Jake watched through tinted windows as families hugged their Trinity graduates. He didn't recognize anyone on his way to Liam and Lily. At last, in the middle of the crowd, the three of them stood in a triangle.

Jake patted Liam on the shoulder.

"Congratulations," Jake said. The word felt oddly long to him. Did anyone else actually say it out loud? All five syllables? He assumed Lily had given Liam the bouquet in his arms. Families around them squeezed together for photos.

"Thanks, Jake," Liam said.

Lily kissed Liam's cheek. He laughed, blushed. Jake felt as if he were intruding. They chatted for a few strained minutes. Jake asked, "So, you feel good?" and "You're all done, then?" among other simple, leading questions. He didn't want to ask about the diploma ceremony that had just ended and draw attention to the fact that he'd missed it. Liam was matriculating at Yale in the fall, but Jake didn't want to talk about that, either. Liam's choice to attend the same schools he had only made his neglect feel even more egregious. But Jake couldn't get past the fact that Liam's existence trivialized his feelings for the only other person who'd ever understood him. How could he have a family with anyone but her?

"How about a picture?" Lily suggested.

She waved the two of them together. Jake hinged his arm around Liam and gave his shoulder a friendly shake. Jake just couldn't act natural around the boy. What was normal, though? How were you supposed to treat your child raised by a woman you barely knew? What were the standards of behav-

ior for that? Jake had never wanted another broken family.
He'd been as sure of that as if the instructions were carved on
his bones. But he found it hard to devote himself to a family
he'd never intended to have.

"Smile, Jake," Lily said.

"Jake?" Lily insisted.

He returned from his flashback.

"His graduation? His show?"

"Right. Sorry. I'll try to go."

"It's next week. Will you or won't you?"

He rubbed his eyes.

"What I don't think you understand is how much you hurt Liam by not showing up."

Her composure was melting. He'd seen that face before. Last year, after Jake missed Liam's show, Lily showed up in his lobby crying. He'd invited her up to Olympus. In his office for the first time, with the door shut, she pointed out that he didn't have a single photo of any friend or family member in there. He'd hung *one* from decades ago with Lionel. Otherwise, the only pictures in his office were of the Messier 15, one of the densest clusters of stars ever discovered, as seen from the Hubble Telescope.

"What else is that important?"

He glanced around Gotta Robota. His heart rate rose to 100 on his Roxster.

"Jake?" Her voice cracked.

"Okay, fine."

"What does that mean?"

"I'll go to the graduation."

"*And* the art show."

Jake fanned himself with his shirt again.

"The art show is more important. Liam is so gifted. He was telling me about the main piece of the show and the ideas behind it. It's about *you*, Jake, his relationship with you . . ." Jake made his hand into a visor over his eyes. Her pain was excruciating. He couldn't hurt her anymore. "He has a rare heart. You haven't even been back to Yale since you graduated—"

"Sorry," Jake said.

He stood.

"For everything. I have a meeting now, but—I'll be at the show."

For the rest of the day, Jake imagined what he might find at "Intertwined." He pictured every possible arrangement of him, Sophie, Lily, and Liam at the show. If the four of them did line up, in half of all cases, he'd stand next to Sophie. He imagined being just a forearm's length away from her. She'd be nodding along to something Liam was saying, stunted by the crowd around them. Her loud mind would be invisible. Would she share her thoughts if he asked for them? Would she want to go for a walk after the show? He pictured a sunny day, and the fantasies absorbed him so completely, whenever he zoned back into the present, he'd find that he'd missed up to a minute of conversation with his analysts.

On his way home, he recalled Dr. Bradley's article. He'd never finished the part about first-love reunions. Now, with a definite plan to return to Yale, it was time. He searched for "Love Interrupted" online, bought the article, and read it almost to the end—

"Boss, we have arrived," Carl blared.

"Carl, stop," Jake said.

The car was still.

"Carl, how long have we been here?"

"Ten minutes, boss."

"All right."

Jake stepped outside into muggy air. His damp neck licked his collar. Inside the lobby, he nodded hello to the doorman before entering his private elevator. In his apartment, lights dawned when he stepped inside. He undressed down to boxer shorts tattered to ruin. With the one piece of his outfit no one saw, Jake didn't pretend. Luxury had never felt like him.

He got into bed itching to finish the article. His room was beautifully quiet. Something about abrupt, unwanted noises chipped away at his soul. All car horns, ringtones, and voices were gone now. His mind could fill the empty space with thought. Jake tapped the final section title on his watch, "Survey Results of 23 First Love Reunions One Decade Later"—enlarging it over his wrist—and read straight through to the end.

A common unknown going into the encounter was how much the other person had changed. Social media only revealed so much. Of the twenty-three former couples surveyed, 74 percent said the other person hadn't changed at all. Their sense of the other was spot-on ten years later. Morning people remained morning people. Shy types stayed shy. The religious ones kept their faith. Personality was quite stable, something Chuck explained in granular detail.

This didn't mean that the ex-couples rekindled their romances. In fact, none did. Only five of the twenty-three couples agreed to meet a second time. Only one of the twenty-three met a third time. There were no fourth encounters. From the interviews that followed, Chuck found that although these people weren't any less compatible, circumstances had changed. Since the couples separated, new children, jobs, interests, and homes had grown between them. Some were tied to cities hundreds of miles apart. No one in Chuck's study felt like they had the chance to do it all over again.

"It's not saying things get better or worse, just messier. Our clothes will fall apart. We'll get old. The things we own will break. Entropy."

CHAPTER 14

Sophie tugged the locked door. Liam's show didn't start for another fifteen minutes. She stepped back and glimpsed her reflection—flowy pink skirt to her ankles, white tee—in the glass walls of the Yale School of Art. She'd considered buying new clothes for today but had gone with classics. She turned her chin side to side. She'd still never pierced her ears.

She opted for a walk around the block. In Yorkside Pizza, families ate sticky pancakes, golden toast. Sophie stopped outside the window. She couldn't remember the last time she'd seen so many babies. A boy in navy-blue overalls yelped in his mom's arms. His New Balance sneakers were doll-size. He had a soft fat layer under his chin. The dad, exuberantly childish, was making faces from the next seat. The baby never stopped squirming. He looked heavy, but Sophie couldn't be sure. She'd never held anyone that size.

Sophie passed more children in Ashley's Ice Cream. The slew of young people made her feel old. For the most part, she liked aging. Life got easier, emotionally. She felt like she could see more at once, that the here and now was not all there was. She passed a girl in a high chair at Blue State with big blue eyes like hers. Sophie still got asked every so often if she had kids. She usually just shook her head. The full truth was that she would have only had children with one man. She didn't crave kids categorically.

Sophie headed back to the art school. She'd been in this building before for a couple of other thesis exhibits. The only spots Sophie *hadn't* been on campus were inside secret society buildings, the windowless town houses nearby. Still, Sophie knew which house belonged to which society. She'd heard enough stories to imagine the rooms and basements. Sophie knew this place. It was part of her.

She opened the doors.

"Professor Jones!" Liam shouted.

He waved with Daya between the entryway and his showroom, beckoning her to follow them inside. Paintings hung in a perfect line around the room. Each canvas was set in a gleaming white frame. Liam stopped in front of the biggest piece of all: the picture from the front of the catalog. The neon bolt was as tall as he was. It glowed electric yellow and blue. Liam's eyes darted between Sophie and the lightning as she read the wall label:

Streamers. *2048*
Oil on canvas

"People are interconnected by invisible forces. Although we have the freedom to think and act, we stick together, like stars on the heavenly arc, with unbreakable connections. These connections cannot be seen, but we can feel them." —Nikola Tesla

During a storm, cloud particles break into positive and negative charges. The negatives shoot down to earth in "streamers," channels that conduct electricity through the air. When streamers connect with positive charges on the ground, the circuit is complete, and lightning strikes. Even though our eye is drawn to the fantastic bolt, streamers are everywhere in a storm. This piece is about the powerful connections we cannot see and the invisibilities that shape our world.

Sophie stood up slowly. She noticed that the comets springing up from the ground had lightsaber blue clockfaces—an unmistakable nod to Roxster. This was Liam's ode to Jake: the connection he felt to a father who wasn't around.

"Wow," Sophie said. "It's—"

"Liam!" Lily called.

She sauntered in wearing stonewashed overalls the same color as Liam's pants, as if they'd been cut from the same enormous denim square. She shone a smile on Daya before she hugged

Liam with all of her strength. She kissed his forehead and then up one side of his face. Liam laughed. Then, at last, Lily and Sophie stood face-to-face, close enough that they could brush each other with the tip of an index finger.

"I'm Lily," she began.

She held out her hand.

"Liam's mom."

Sophie felt Lily's warmth. It was in this woman's kind smile, the number of times she'd kissed Liam in a row, and how she kept a hand on his shoulder now.

"Sophie Jones," Sophie said.

They shook hands.

Sophie cleared her throat.

"I taught Liam physics," she explained.

"She did more than that," Liam said.

He gestured at the painting.

"Oh, *Liam*," Lily gushed. "It's a masterpiece." The four of them stood as points in a jagged hemisphere around it. "I love how weightless it is." Lily swirled her fingers inches above a gray whirl in the sky. "Who else could make a storm so light? You amaze me."

"Thanks, Mom," Liam said. "Sophie actually helped with the idea."

Outside the Yale School of Art at that moment, heat wrinkled the air above the black hood of Jake's car. He wore a crewneck over gray jeans, one suit jacket away from his usual outfit. He'd considered wearing something different—special—but, then again, this was who he was. It was appropriate. He wasn't trying to hide.

He didn't pray or worship any oracle in particular, but that morning, he'd read his horoscope. He'd felt so wide open inside and unsteady on his feet that he had the unusual desire to ask for help from beyond the human world. Janice was Catholic, but the church had never stuck with him. He didn't know where else to turn. There was wisdom in the stars, wasn't there? So, he read the advice meant for every Sagittarius: "Beware of strong emotions on this day. Your best tools will be clear thinking, patience, and staying calm." It was vague, but the words soothed him. Jake felt a flickering connection to something eternal and unbreakable.

He looked out his window at the city where he'd spent the most formative years of his life. So far, New Haven was just like he remembered. A teen walked by carrying volumes of Thoreau, Emerson, and Whitman. From here, Jake saw the building where he'd had a history class on the Cold War. He imagined its syllabus unchanged. Nearby, Jake had taken Psych 101, where he'd learned about immersion therapy for phobias. That treatment required people to confront what they feared, in virtual reality or in the real world. Someone who was afraid of crowds might face a mob in a simulation—or someone afraid of rejection might face the woman he loved. Jake opened the door. He put sunglasses on, took them off, and then left them on the seat folded into the glasses equivalent of the fetal position.

He stepped onto the sidewalk.

The art building glimmered.

As Jake walked toward it, step by step, he'd never felt more vulnerable. His physical awareness was at an all-time high. When he swallowed, he felt his entire existence in his throat. A loop of breaths linked him tenuously to life. He was acutely aware that he had no special powers, only soft tissue and breakable bones. He was imperfect. He'd hurt other people with his selfishness and neglect. Like many others, he'd fallen in love and never forgotten it. He was just a man.

He stepped inside.

The gallery bustled.

A teen handed him a catalog. Jake rolled it into a tube and squeezed it at his side. He was head and shoulders above almost everyone else. Liam stood twenty feet away talking to Lily, Daya, and . . . Sophie. Finally. They were in the same room. His veins flooded with euphoria and terror. He needed to be closer to her, feared she didn't feel the same way. After all, his flaws had had fifty-five years to emerge. He'd abandoned her and built a separate, broken family—but he did love her. Deeply, singularly. His life wasn't perfect, but his love for her was. She stood sideways to him. He walked toward her. Her profile was small. He could've covered it with his thumb. Back when they were in college, he used to watch her listen to their professor, her expression kindly curious. Now, an arm's length in front of him, she wore an expression just as kind, just as curious. She was still Sophie. His feelings for her had never changed.

"Jake," Liam said.

Lily and Daya turned.

Sophie swiveled tick by tick, slow as a clock's second hand. A row of ceiling lights shone on them now face-to-face. His dark eyes tagged her blue.

"Hi, Sophie."

His heart throbbed. Ecstasy, fear. He was thrilled to be re-united, horrified she might not be. The moment was delicate, precarious. She could end it all with a slight shake of her head, or with a goodbye and a sudden rush to be somewhere else. He waited and—her gaze didn't leave him. Her expression was warm, hopeful. Optimistic, even.

"You recognize me?" she asked.

"Everything's the same."

Her, his heart.

He cleared his throat.

He had to change the subject before he lost composure.

"Well," he said. "How about a tour?"

Liam guided them through the gallery. All three portraits of Daya blended her limbs into flowers, ferns, and other greenery. Daya blushed when Liam said he wanted the plant theme to evoke fertility. As Liam explained each piece, he glanced more often at Jake than at anyone else. Jake didn't interject. He had no thoughts to share or questions to ask. His mind felt scram-bled and useless. All he could do was feel: hopeful, vulnerable, and observant. Throughout the tour, he and Sophie stayed side by side, only an inch of space between them. Never touching, never far. He beheld every one of her details. Eventually, he caught her eye for an electric millisecond as Lily gushed over *My Mom the Miracle Tree*. They ended at *Streamer*s. Liam stood in front of the painting, obscuring it, with his arms across his chest.

"Thank you for—" Liam started.

"What about this one?" Jake interrupted. "This is the cover, right?"

Liam nodded, stepped aside.

"Well," he started warily. "It captures 'streamers,' which are an invisible, powerful presence during a storm. This piece takes that idea and finds an analogy in relationships. Sometimes, you have a powerful bond with someone who isn't around. Just like streamers, two people can have something charged, out of sight, connected."

Sophie, Lily, and Daya were quiet. Everywhere else, chatty visitors milled about the space. The crowd cinched in groups of three or four. A few leaned toward particular works, backs hunched, noses dangerously close to the paint.

"That's wise," Jake said.

"Thank you."

Lily smiled proudly.

"And thank you all for coming," Liam said.

"Can I take you two to lunch later, sweetheart?" Lily asked.

"Yes!" Daya interjected.

"Perfect," Liam agreed.

Lily looked at Jake.

"Are you free to join?" she asked him.

Jake hadn't spent a weekday out of the office in years. His dark desk at Olympus, longer than his wingspan and finished in midnight java, was his home. His original team of four plus Tawny all still worked for him. Lionel hadn't retired, either. He came to One Madison in a suit and tie every day with the appetite of his teenage self, still eager for that next best idea. Today, Jake didn't have a call he needed to take or a meeting he needed to attend. His schedule was in his own hands. Yes, he'd be "free to join," but the idea of a lunch break was so strange to him—in such unfamiliar territory—that he couldn't answer.

"Anyway." Liam put everyone out of their discomfort. "It really was great to see you."

Jake squeezed the catalog.

"I'll be here tomorrow," he said.

Liam smiled, thanked him.

Jake and Sophie left at the same time. They walked as close as if they were in the middle of a conversation. Gallery chatter faded step by step. Jake summoned the elevator.

"Your son," Sophie said, "is a really good man."

Inside the elevator, the only sound was their breathing. Sophie remained acutely aware of Jake's body just an inch away. In a flashback, she unzipped her backpack next to him in Bass. She imagined how their elbows might graze if she got lost in her own mind, her body forgotten. The vision faded.

Her love for him remained. Seconds later, they came to a stop. Stepped outside. Faced each other in the bright morning. The small veins under Jake's eyes were bigger now. They protruded like wrinkles turned inside out. His jawline was softer without being any less lean. She would know his face anywhere. Her love for him was timeless.

"Do you want to take a walk?" Jake asked.

His tone was not presumptive.

She nodded.

They strolled up Hillhouse past the firs.

"This is the most I've been outdoors in a while," Jake said.

They walked.

Rays of sunlight cast spiderweb patterns on the sidewalk.

"What'd you think of the show?" Sophie asked.

He smirked and laughed quietly.

Sophie looked around for what had happened.

"You won't believe me," he said.

"What?"

"I had a hard time focusing."

They passed the psychology building where they'd met. There, they'd learned the concept of social judgment. When you met someone, you instantly sized up two qualities: competence and warmth. On those two axes, you plotted every first encounter. But Jake believed he could judge a third dimension: what people wanted from him. His teachers had wanted him to make them feel important. His mom had wanted him to succeed. Most people wanted his money. With Sophie, though, he never knew. She didn't seem to want anything from him. He couldn't sense any agenda. She was the first person he'd ever met whose affection was truly free.

They reached the top of Science Hill by the brick-and-metal Kline Biology Tower. It stood sixteen floors high, prominent as an obelisk. They sat next to each other at a picnic table half a football field away from the Sloane Physics Lab. They could see into Kline's ground-floor café and over the rest of campus below.

"Is it what you remembered?" she asked.

"You are."

"Jake."

Their battered table was riddled with carved initials, scratches of every width, tree rings, and a crack down the middle that appeared to split the table in slow motion. Jake scratched the surface and flicked a microscopic wood chip into the quad.

"Most people, when they get older, they get harder," he said. "You didn't."

"Jake."

"What?"

"Go slow."

A young couple sat at another picnic table and shared two sandwiches out of plastic to-go boxes, one half for each person. Jake reached for her hand. She traced a figure eight around two of his knuckles with her thumb.

"I can't believe I let you go," he said.

She shook her head.

"You didn't," she said.

He squinted.

"That's what I proved," she said.

"You proved block theory."

"Because I felt you with me when you were gone. I kept walking into visions of us in college as if those moments were happening now. Then, when I read about block theory . . . I just knew. That was it. That was true." The idea had been there all along in the poetry she loved most. *"Love rests on no foundation . . . with no beginning or end." "Lovers don't finally meet somewhere. They're in each other all along." "Goodbyes are only for those who love with their eyes. Because for those who love with heart and soul there is no such thing as separation."* The spirit of block theory had been in all of Jake's music celebrating timeless connections.

"I had those visions too."

He looked at his watchband.

"Did you ever . . . see the future?" he asked.

"No, why? Did you?"

He nodded.

"What'd you see?" she asked.

In his mind, the sun had set. Their house was like Sophie's childhood home, surrounded by trees. Her silhouette shaded a yellow window in the library.

Jake squeezed her hand.

"Us."

He reflected.

"And, now that I think about it, some of my ideas. Sometimes at work, I saw companies taking off before everyone else did. They were like visual gut feelings. I thought they might've been more than that, but . . . I don't know, I thought that would've been impossible."

"Is that how you picked Roxster?"

He shook his head.

"No, I picked that for you. Roxster had always funded research on time. My biggest decisions were always for you, Sophie." He didn't want to waste more time. "How do you feel about New York?"

"What?"

"I can't go back without you."

Sophie's blue eyes grew.

"It's changed since we've been there," he went on. "Not like this." He pointed around Science Hill. As her head swiveled, he imagined them in a furnished version of his apartment. "I should've asked you sooner. I should've come back decades ago. But I heard this interview . . . I thought you had more to prove. I should've just come back."

Sophie squinted in confusion.

"With the *Yale Daily News*? Your 'other ideas'? I didn't want to get in the way."

Sophie's head slanted. She didn't disagree.

"You still do have other ideas," he realized.

He waited.

"What are they?" he asked.

She picked one.

"When you fall in love, you see time the way it truly is. That's the simple version of a bigger idea. The full truth is more complex than that. Have you ever heard of supersymmetry?" Jake shook his head. "It's the idea that every particle has a partner, called its 'superpartner.' No one's ever seen one. Or measured one. But they balance important equations that don't make sense without them." Jake nodded along. "Some say superpartners are components of dark matter, the parts of the universe we can't see, and—"

"And?"

"I think these partners exist. More than that, I think they exist at every mass. I think everyone has a superpartner—a configuration of mass and energy—that connects them to the world beyond what we can see." She squeezed Jake's hand. "We form these intense connections with our superpartners, and they bring us closer to reality. It's why we saw time as it actually is. I think this is the idea some people try to capture with the term *soul mate*, but it's so much greater than that. It's closer to a portal. A window. To everything we haven't measured. We have real, physiological reactions to being around them. They balance us."

Jake wrapped his mind around the idea.

"So why didn't you explore that?"

"I lost interest after block theory."

"Why?"

"I trusted myself. I didn't need to prove it to know it was true."

Science Hill was quiet.

"You still have time to pursue it," he said.

He withdrew his hand.

Sophie realized his intention: to leave in hopes she'd continue to work.

"Jake," she said, "that's not how I want to spend my life. That's not even the most important idea. Not even close." Urgency warped her pace. She spoke faster. "It's not about the mind. The most valuable insight of my life has been that the best use of time is to love. It's not a sophisticated idea, and that's exactly the point. People overvalue intellect. Life should be lived from the heart." He appeared deeply thoughtful. "So, whenever I have the choice, I should spend my time with other people. Even if that means I leave less of a mark on the world at large." It was why she still taught. She'd matured into the most social version of herself: teaching classes, holding office hours, seeing the Malchiks and their friends, and visiting her parents. She was unfailingly kind. She'd never stopped loving Jake.

He exhaled a long breath.

He looked prepared to deliver bad news.

"Jake, please don't make any rash decisions. We don't need to solve everything today. We'll see each other tomorrow. You'll be clearheaded by then."

"I love you," he said.

"I know."

CHAPTER 15

Sophie walked down Hillhouse in blazing sunlight, drifting in step with dozens of families. Their sound waves collided around her. Laughs, shrieks, and chatter competed for air as everyone headed to Cross Campus for the graduation ceremony.

She hadn't spoken to Jake yet, even though they'd exchanged phone numbers.

He would be there, right? She stopped at the open gates. Thousands of folding chairs faced a stage in front of Sterling Library. The crowd stunned her into a standstill. Only fifteen minutes remained until the procession. The front section stayed empty awaiting the graduates. She spotted her parents, Jolene, and the Malchiks in the section closest to Hopper College.

She texted him: Jake?

Graduates approached down her side of the street. Their black hems swished around their ankles. Seniors would pass her on their way to enter the other side of the quad.

She looked at her watch.

"Sophie!"

It took her a moment to locate the noise.

Liam trotted toward her in full cap and gown.

"You're not going to believe this," he said.

"What?"

The line trudged on without him.

"The Davis Gallery wants to represent me." The Davis Gallery? "It's a major gallery in New York City. Marshall Davis was at my show yesterday." Liam shook his head in awe. "My mom said Jake asked him to come. I can't tell you how happy I am."

"That's fantastic!"

"I just found out. He loves *Streamers*."

Sophie hugged him. Liam laughed, and when he pulled away, he kept his hands on her shoulders. His eyes had stars in them.

"You have to come see it in New York," he insisted.

"Of course."

"Thank you. For everything."

His graduation cap accentuated his ears, which stuck out farther from his head than usual.

"I've gotta run," he said.

His smile touched her as he jogged back to his place in line, his robe dancing behind him. She held her own hand and watched him until he disappeared.

* * *

Jake was sitting in his hotel room just a block away. He hunched forward on the sofa in the same outfit he'd worn to Liam's show. His elbows pressed into his knees. His fists propped his chin. Liam's ceremony would start any minute. Jake hadn't chosen to skip it, but he hadn't yet decided to go. He didn't know if he could see Sophie again. The question wasn't whether he and Sophie loved each other. It was whether he needed to be with the one he loved. He kept replaying snippets from their talk yesterday. All night long, he'd worded and reworded dozens of things he could've said. After she told him, *"Even if that means I leave less of a mark on the world at large,"* he could've added, "But you'll never see yourself the way I do. You'll never know how hard it would be to live with your light just—out."

"The most valuable insight of my life has been that the best use of time is to love."

At the time, Jake had been trying to grasp supersymmetry— thinking that it explained the pull between them, that they were each other's superpartner, and their relationship had connected them both to true reality—so he hadn't paid full attention to what she'd said. Jake stood up fast and felt woozy. He sat back down.

"The best use of time is to love."

Finally, he understood. If he really did respect her once-in-a-century genius, he'd have to honor her conclusion that, in things that really mattered, the mind didn't matter at all. The answers weren't in the head, they were in the heart. People should spend their precious time loving one another. He laughed. He really could bring her back to New York. In his apartment, they could hang whatever she wanted on the walls.

He left the hotel.

On his way to Cross Campus, he passed their old double in Berkeley and looked up at the window. Sophomore year, the day before classes started, they'd hoisted the mattress and headboard from one bedroom into the other and combined them. Weeks into the semester, they still hadn't adjusted to the extra space. They slept together in only one of the two beds. Every morning, they woke up to see a twin's width of wasted sheets and unused pillows beyond Sophie. Even on the rare night when they started out on opposite sides, in an attempt to enjoy the extravagance of two whole beds, they woke up close together in a narrow lane.

"Why can't we use our bed right?" Sophie groaned one morning.

"Because we're looking for each other in our sleep," Jake said.

Jake passed their hammock.

He passed their dining hall.

He made his way through the audience amidst thunderous applause. The graduation ceremony had just begun. Everyone in the crowd cheered on their feet as the procession snaked through rows of chairs in the front. Jake spotted her between her parents and an empty seat. His heart raced as he approached. All this time, he'd thought she'd lost herself. Really, she'd been living out her greatest discovery.

Their eyes met.

"Thanks," he whispered as everyone sat.

He gestured to the vacant seat.

"Of course," she said.

He kissed her cheek.

"I love you," she said.

"I know."

ACKNOWLEDGMENTS

Special thanks to Eve Attermann at William Morris Endeavor for believing in me from the start and for leading the charge through two dream-come-true processes. I am extremely grateful for your guidance and savvy! This book also wouldn't be possible without Kaitlin Olson, my best first reader and miracle-working editor at Atria Books. It is a complete joy to work with you, Megan Rudloff, and Isabel DaSilva at Atria.

Thank you to Zibby Owens, of the *Moms Don't Have Time to Read Books* podcast, and Kyle Owens, of Morning Moon Productions, for hosting memorable literary salons, for creating a vibrant community of authors and readers in New York City, and for including me in that community. I am also grateful to Kevin Warsh and Jane Lauder for supporting the launch of *Breathe In, Cash Out: A Novel*, and for being incredible mentors to me for years.

Thank you to Dan Brown for generously sharing his time

with me during my first book tour, and for imparting invaluable advice on writing.

Thank you to Carolyn Brody and Jesse Bartel at BookHampton; to Monica Lerch at Kramerbooks & Afterwords in Washington, DC; to Book Soup in Los Angeles; to Nina Barrett at Bookends & Beginnings in Evanston, Ilinois; to Elissa Sweet from the Savoy Bookshop & Café in Westerly, Rhode Island; to Suzanne Leopold of @SuzyApprovedBookReviews; to Katie Taylor of @The_Grateful_Read; to Joan Hamburg, of *The Joan Hamburg Show* on 77 WABC; to my extraordinarily talented copyeditor Polly Watson; and to my Yale English professor Alfred Guy. I appreciate how you've supported me and how you continue to share your love of great books.

Thank you to the yogis who inspired me while I was still in finance and gave me the courage to follow my dreams: Neyu @Neyu_Ma and Janice @JaniceLiou.

I benefited from the counsel of Tom Distler at Brooks & Distler.

Last but not least, thank you to my family—Jody, both Emils, and Parker—for their unconditional love and encouragement. Thank you also to the Alexandres for rallying around each book with terrific enthusiasm and for always being so kind.

Thank you most to Dave, my everything.

ABOUT THE AUTHOR

Madeleine Henry is the author of two novels, including *Breathe In, Cash Out*. She has appeared on NBC, WABC, *The Jenny McCarthy Show*, and Inspire Living. She has been featured in the *New York Post*, *Parade*, and Observer Media. Previously, she worked at Goldman Sachs and in investment management after graduating from Yale in 2014. She shares more information about her life on @MadeleineHenryYoga and about her upcoming third novel on @FoodFightBook.

THE

LOVE PROOF

MADELEINE HENRY

This reading group guide for The Love Proof *includes an introduction, discussion questions, ideas for enhancing your book club,
and a Q & A with the author. The suggested questions are intended
to help your reading group find new and interesting angles and
topics for your discussion. We hope that these ideas will enrich your
conversation and increase your enjoyment of the book.*

INTRODUCTION

In *The Love Proof*, a brilliant physics prodigy studying the nature of time embarks on a journey to prove that those we love are always connected to us.

Sophie Jones is on track to unlock the secrets of the universe. But when she meets Jake Kristopher during their first week at Yale, they instantly feel a deep connection, as if they've known each other before. Quickly, they become a couple. Slowly, their love lures Sophie away from school.

When a shocking development forces Sophie into a new reality, she returns to physics to make sense of her world. She grapples with life's big questions, including how to cope with unexpected change and loss. Inspired by her connection with Jake, Sophie throws herself into her studies, determined to prove that true loves belong together in all realities.

QUESTIONS FOR DISCUSSION

1. The epigraph of this novel focuses on the power of connection. How does this theme recur throughout the novel? How do these words set up what is to come? After having finished the novel, has your perspective on connection changed?

2. Early on, Professor Malchik describes Sophie's talent to his son using a video game metaphor, explaining that he is coaching her even though she hasn't played the game because "you know, really know, that with your help, she'll not only pass the highest level you've ever seen, she will win the game" (p. 7). Reflect on Professor Malchik and Sophie's relationship. As a coach, does he succeed at helping her win this game? Why or why not?

3. Chapters 2 and 3 focus on Sophie's and Jake's early lives. How are they similar? How are they different? How do their backgrounds bring them together and influence their trajectories throughout the novel?

4. In part one, Sophie is often described in childlike terms. She's small and loves candy (p. 66). Why do you think this is? What does it say about her character?

5. By the end of freshman year, Jake has an internship in finance and Sophie has decided to work at Free People, saying she's taken a retail job to free her mind for larger questions, but she notes internally that "the truth was that she cared less and less about the questions that used to keep her up at night: What really controls us? What plucks the strings of the universe? What is the real power of love?" (p. 105). How does the progression of Jake and Sophie's relationship draw her away from her studies and previous interests? What reaction did you have to this revelation?

6. When Sophie meets Lionel Padington for the first time, she announces that "'the least understood, most important thing in the world is love.'" (p. 113). Jake finds himself unsettled and embarrassed by Sophie's words to his mentor, and he notes that their relationship has changed her. How does this scene change Jake's perception of Sophie?

7. Shortly after graduation and after founding Olympus Capital, Jake blindsides Sophie by breaking up with her, noting that "'this is a critical period for you, too. Now's the time to set up the rest of our lives.'" (p. 140). Throughout their relationship, Jake is haunted by his mother's warning: "'If she's in the way of your dream, she's not the one.'" (p. 95). Why does Jake choose this moment to insist that he and Sophie go in different directions?

8. Jake's nickname is Einstein, something Sophie used to be called, for his objectively genius results. But his flagship investment is Roxster, which he has chosen not just for its potential, but because it also funds research at institutions studying the nature of time, connecting him to Sophie (pp. 183–84). What does this emotionally driven investment reveal about Jake's character?

9. Although Sophie is energized by her graduate school work, she struggles with the questions she wants to answer, until an innocuous comment from Benji Malchik at the end of the New Haven Half Marathon, which causes her to consider "*transformation*—that was it" (p. 189). What leads to Sophie's insight at that moment?

10. After Sophie returns to Yale, Professor Malchik becomes a mentor and confidant to her, inviting her into the family. What effect does the Malchik family have on Sophie's

personal and professional life? Why do you believe she names her famous theorem after Professor Malchik?

11. When Jake finds out what Sophie has accomplished, he sets out to contact her, but deletes his email after watching a video where a reporter asks her what's next and Sophie says, "'I have some ideas'" (p. 193), making him believe Sophie has more to discover. Why does Jake feel that he would stand in the way of Sophie's greatness? What might have happened had Jake sent that email?

12. The novel jumps forward twenty-five years, to when Sophie— now a professor—meets Jake's son, Liam (p. 201). Why do you believe the author made the choice to accelerate the timeline, moving quickly from present to future?

13. Liam has trouble with physics, and Sophie illustrates what makes physics exciting by telling him about streamers: "'The electricity in the air before lightning strikes? My point is that you can't see any of these things, but you can feel them, and physics can prove them to you. You can't see them, but physics shows you they're there'" (p. 224). How does this relate to Sophie's work on the concept of time? Why does Liam choose to use streamers as the inspiration for a piece in his senior show?

14. At the end of the novel, Sophie tells Jake that she arrived at block theory "because I felt you with me when you were

gone" (p. 264). What inspires the other ideas Sophie had, which she no longer felt she had to prove? What conclusions does she draw, both from theories like supersymmetry, and from her own lack of interest in proving them?

15. Throughout the novel, Jake and Sophie repeat, "I love you," and, "I know," which also concludes the novel (p. 273). How does this exchange underscore the theme of intuition? How does this fit into what Sophie discovers about block theory?

ENHANCE YOUR BOOK CLUB

1. Spend some time researching block theory, then discuss with your group. Had you encountered this concept before, either in an academic or fictional setting? Does it ring true for you?

2. "Equation by equation, Sophie transformed everything into Fourier space. She filled page after page, front and back. She didn't feel like she was doing math. She was telling the world what it had felt like to be her. This was where her intuition had led" (p. 190). After Jake and Sophie break up, she trusts her gut feeling that he's still with her, which leads her to prove block theory. Do you believe that intuition is a trustworthy guide in life? Why or why not? Has there been a particular crossroad when you trusted your intuition completely?

3. "Of course, no one ever wanted to move on. No one ever wanted to fall in love again after they gave their heart away to someone who didn't come back" (p. 166). In this book, Sophie does not "move on"—and neither does Jake. Have you or someone you know ever experienced a love like this?

4. Visit the author's website to learn more about Madeleine's work and listen to the music that she selected to pair with this book.

A CONVERSATION WITH MADELEINE HENRY

What do you hope readers take away from this story?
The Love Proof is about the love that endures after a relationship ends. It captures the sentiment of *I still care about you. I know you still care about me. I still feel you with me, sense you with me wherever I go.* Feelings don't leave just because people do.

I hope that readers find this to be a beautiful story, not just in the ideas that emerge from the text—most importantly, that we're always connected to the people we love—but down to the sentence level. I view this book as a tribute to the most beautiful parts of human character, too. It highlights noble traits including dedication, loyalty, hard work, and unconditional, timeless love. I hope it all comes together in a really gorgeous and stimulating way.

Your first novel was an incisive satire of both the banking and yoga worlds. *The Love Proof* **is a heartfelt love story. What prompted this change in direction? Do you see similarities between these two novels?**

I think of my books as pieces in a bigger, cohesive work. In *Breathe In, Cash Out*, Allegra Cobb is a tense Princeton grad who's palpably suffering in her office job. What's missing from her life? My next books answer that question. Each is a story on its own, and altogether, they make up a broader narrative about what's truly meaningful and satisfying. Each is structured around a core theme, and together they reveal what Allegra needed to find joy. In *The Love Proof*, the core idea is connection. In my next book, *Food Fight*, it's self-compassion. In the following story, *Begin with a Broken Heart*, it's faith.

The Love Proof and *Breathe In, Cash Out* do have more in common, though, than just comprising the same mosaic. First, they're both emotionally autobiographical. *Breathe In, Cash Out* captures the feeling of a stifling job, working in a place that's strangling your soul. *The Love Proof* is a portrayal of loss, grief, and not-letting-go in a way that's also authentic. Both books have pulses. Second, both draw from yoga, Zen, and New Age ideas. While Allegra aspires to these ideals, Sophie actually manifests them. Some yogis try to live without ego, meaning they don't identify with the impermanent parts of their life. Sophie, to me, is egoless. She doesn't want attention or aspire to achievement. She is truly humble.

Jake and Sophie meet at Yale, which you also attended. What was it like to depict the campus in a work of fiction?

It was fun! It seemed fitting to set the story at Yale because it's a place where change is less frequent, where time feels like it's passing at a different rate, and that's a theme in this book.

This novel draws on a lot of different disciplines, including physics, finance, and art. Each character is defined by his or her passion for a subject. Is that something you were conscious of as you were writing?

Interesting! I suppose that emerges because that's how I've been for a lot of my life. I tend to have one project at a time that I'm very passionate about, and maybe that oozes into my characters. They focus on one thing or a small subset of things because I do, too.

Did anything—plot or characters—surprise you while writing the book?

I'm surprised that this story takes place over a lifetime, which is much more ambitious in scope than my first book. Whenever I write, I'm surprised that my work always attempts to be so substantial and intense when in person I feel very unassuming. The intention of this book really is significant, in that I wanted to memorialize and communicate a very intense feeling of permanent connection in a way that did it justice. I'm surprised that the main characters in this story are all so inward-looking and consumed by their own internal battles. I'm surprised at how short the book is, relative to what I try to accomplish within it.

What was your favorite scene to write? Which was the hardest?
My favorite to write was when Professor Malchik tells Sophie about his lost daughter. It came through me very quickly. As it was happening, I felt more like a reader than a writer. I remember when Professor Malchik said, "I think she still has the clothes," before I thought the phrase, which was very moving. Then he said Annie's name before I anticipated it. I didn't edit that scene much after the first draft. It just worked.

Structuring the scene when Sophie talks to Liam for the first time was hard because I wanted to make time slow down literally on the page. I wanted to communicate a sense of altered reality. How was I supposed to do that? I spent a lot of time thinking about it.

Is there a character that you identify with in the novel?
Every character has parts of me in them. I'm like Jake because I can be singularly focused and content alone. I'm like Sophie because I can be youthfully idealistic. I'm like Professor Malchik because I used to expect my work to complete me. That being said, the character I identify with *most* is Sophie. She's kind and loyal—to Jake, to her gut, to her dream.

At the end of the novel, Jake notes that "if he really did respect her once-in-a century genius, he'd have to honor her conclusion that, in things that really mattered, the mind didn't matter at all. The answers weren't in the head, they

were in the heart" (p. 271). Obviously, these are your own words. What does this message mean to you?

Sophie thinks that a simple life with Jake is the most fulfilling version of her time on earth. Achievement doesn't feed her soul. Connection does.

Does this resonate with me? Yes.

The big difference between Sophie's view of love and mine is that she's very *couple*-focused, while I'm more *family*-oriented. She is so focused on pouring all of her love into one person, but I see a bigger world than that. I think that's because, for most of the book, she's younger than I am. Younger women are more concerned with romantic love and finding a partner. Now that I'm with my partner, I view us as a family that can grow and explore the world together—not as a twosome who can hide together from everyone else.

Another way I've aged slightly out of her perspective is in my appreciation for imperfections. This book sees people through an idealistic lens, but I'm at a point in my life where I'm having more warmth for flaws and weaknesses. I bring that perspective into my next book, *Food Fight*, which embraces full people more tenderly. You don't need to be perfect to be loved by others, and, no matter what, you can always love yourself.